a
LOCKET
of
HERMES

ADAM CRAIG

LIQUORICE
FISH BOOKS

Published by Liquorice Fish Books
an imprint of Cinnamon Press,
Office 49019, PO Box 92, Cardiff, CF11 1NB
www.cinnamonpress.com

Print Edition ISBN 978-1-911540-13-7

British Library Cataloguing in Publication Data. A CIP record for this book can be obtained from the British Library.

Designed and typeset by Liquorice Fish Books.

Liquorice Fish Books is represented by Inpress.

to Patrick — a skein in the Golden Thread,

Tracey, for her company along the way,

and

to Jan, always

a LOCKET of
HERMES

I
NIGRADO

ANOTHER DAY CAME, dressed in widower's black, to lead Tristram along too-familiar streets, past people blank and severe as the stone buildings crowding closer with each step, day again prodding Tristram down that long road to the post office. *Today, I'm sure*, Tristram had told his landlord, one hand, guilty as any sneak thief, straying towards his jacket pocket, although it knew well what rested there. *Today*, he had assured himself as he left the tall rooming house, day's black as black as the sun overhead, sun watching him make this journey through the rattle of tram and shrill of motorcar horn, past men hurrying from the news in the daily papers folded neatly under their arms, past stately Grande Dames wafting along the boulevards like dreams of old empire, and young children, alone or shepherded by nannies, stranded on street corners, unsure whether to go forward into futures uncertain or back into pasts that hardly laid claim over them. Tristram, through it all, walking slowly, day a black armband only he could see. Tristram clasping one hand in the other as he waited for horse and dray to plod aside.

It was, amongst other things, the feast day of Saints Cyril and Methodius, 1930, although Tristram was no longer sure of time and date, only place—the post office ahead, all futures opening with the parting of its doors.

The young man behind the grill gave no sign of recognition, although Tristram had spoken to him several times before, come to this place each day it was open. Young man listening without expression to broken Hungarian giving way German, to a smattering of French, as Tristram made request, counted coins—one, two, five, denominations small yet mounting to the right total. The floor of the post office was hard and cold through thin cardboard soles, cheap shoes one day old.

Don't think of these things, Tristram reminded himself as he waited for the operator to dial the number, phone booth haunted by a faint perfume-ghost of its last occupant, which pressed close to listen to whir and tick on the line, her expression unreadable when the operator finally returned.

'*Ja, danka.*'

Outside, the widower day pressed its face against the glass.

Tristram closed his eyes and felt the weight of four months bear down on this one point—post office, phone booth, the telephone ringing at the far end of the line. His free hand touched the breast of his jacket, feeling through the cloth for a trace of what rested in the pocket beneath. He almost missed the voice repeating, 'Hello?'

'Oh, Villiers,' he stammered. 'My heavens, it's good to hear— Yes, old man, that's right, it is me and it has been a long— Hm? Well, that's, that's something of a tale and I'd be happy to tell—'

Villiers. Images overlaid: a man so young he was hardly old enough to grow the moustache he spent so much time grooming; a man, his age unimportant, hardly able to support himself against the trench wall as they waited for the whistle, their terror shared; a man older, no longer gaunt but full and confident, affluent.

'No,' Tristram managed to interrupt, 'I'm afraid I've not kept up with the news and that's rather why I'm telephoning… Bank, yes, yes, and— No, Villiers, Hungary, but if I may—'

Four months. Each day passing under the gaze of a sun turned black and each night barren. Each day given an extra taint by the forestalling of this call. All futures paused, breaths held while this voice, grown thick on brandy and cigars, spoke over a long distance telephone line. Spoke without listening, certainly without understanding.

'Pardon me, Villiers, but truly, old man, if I had… I grant that these are difficult times, which was why— Which was why…'

His voice caught, pleading as he never imagined he would have to. Hand straying to jacket breast as his mind strayed back, to a wedding day, Villiers still a young man in years, Tristram self-conscious in morning suit, eschewing the medals some guests chose to sport, a black armband almost invisible on the sleeve of his coat. Handing Villiers the ring that would go on the bride's finger. Tears buried so there was no chance they might spoil his friend's great day.

'A small loan—' Tears ran down Tristram's face as he held the receiver tightly against his ear. 'Villiers? Villiers…?'

Dial tone. Good shoes pawned to pay for nothing more than this broken connection and an end to all futures.

There was once a tall house that stood at the end of a small road tucked inside Báthori utca, in Budapest. War and uprising, occupations and liberations, the hardships between: each has helped erased road and house so well, no trace of either remains, as if they had been nothing but dream or a cloud's shadow. To Tristram, that February morning, the house was hard and reproachful, its many windows unblinking as he walked from Báthori down the small road that had no name and little claim on the map. The house guessed his secrets.

Passing the latch key from hand to hand; a deep breath when he at last eased open the door, the hinges silent—tall house still. Tristram ducked inside, gently closing the door and stealing past the landlord's ground floor rooms to mount the stone stairs. An urge to run climbed behind him, pushing at his back. At last, the door to Tristram's room appeared over the lip of the very last landing. Urge to run transforming the last few steps into a single, ungainly bound. Key turning— *Quietly*, Tristram urged—and the door beginning to open. He relaxed.

'Ah, my young sir, I am happy to see you. Are you well? Have you had news?'

Tristram startled back.

His landlord stepped from the empty room next door, face benign as he nodded greetings, excusing himself as he locked the door to the untenanted room, before turning his attention back to Tristram:

'Good news, I trust?'

11

Tone never less than kindly, as unchanging as the landlord's dove grey, double-breasted suit, impeccable and incongruous for someone who looked after such a modest boarding house. Always a single smirch on the landlord's white spats. Always the left cuff of his shirt was frayed.

'I...'

'Yes?' His landlord smiled encouragingly, one eyebrow raised in polite enquiry.

'I'm sorry to say...' One hand clung tightly to the other, both hidden behind Tristram's back. He coughed, glanced away. Aware of how this might appear, he shook his head and stood straighter, thinking of the silence after the last artillery shell had detonated, and the certainty that the whistles would sound at any moment; and so thinking of Vivien, wanting to remember exactly the sound of her laugh and finding only a silence into which Tristram said, 'I'm afraid I've heard nothing, mein Herr. Sadly, nothing. But I am sure my employers will be in touch any day now. And let me say once again how grateful I am for your tolerance and forbearance—'

'Please, please, not at all, young sir.' The landlord waved away Tristram's words, seemingly embarrassed. 'The world in turmoil, banks and fortunes vanishing overnight, and you caught up in it all, unwillingly, as you are—what, young sir, what more can one do?'

'Still, I am awfully grateful, sir, and I'm very aware—' Tristram felt his hands tighten— 'that I owe you rent in addition to gratitude and I—' He swallowed. 'And I can only apologise again that my superiors have not been able to offer anything beyond reassurances so far.'

'Yes, yes, of course, young sir, of course.' The landlord in dove grey suit, frayed cuffs and dirty spats, patted Tristram's arm as he turned towards the stairs. 'Trying times,' he repeated several times as he started downwards.

Tristram sagged against the door to his room, sweat prickling forehead and palms. *How many more times?* But called down the stairs, 'Thank you, sir, I'm sure tomorrow...' and tried to believe in nothing so much as another day's dawning under a sun as black as iron.

'Of course, young sir.'

'I'm sure tomorrow,' Tristram repeated, opening his door.

'Of course. And yet, young sir—'

No time to slip into the room. No time to close the door and pretend he had not heard, landlord reappearing on the landing.

'I thought, perhaps, the other day, these four days past, in fact...?'

'I'm... sorry?'

'You remember, dear young sir. You returned from your daily trip to the post office in a state of some emotion. I saw you.' Expression not wavering and his tone no different to moments ago, yet the smile appeared harsh on the landlord's face and there was an edge to the words that spread a chill through Tristram's stomach. 'I watched, from my window at the front of the house, as you paced up and down, talking to yourself, words only sounds through the glass but I heard their tone and I thought you had word from your employers and that word carried bad news. Yet here we are, days and several more visits to the post office later and you tell me you have heard nothing, not word nor telegram, simply nothing.'

Smile no longer kindly.

Tristram wanted the safety of his room, to slam the door in the landlord's face. But there was no retreat. There was only to advance and survive.

'It was a memory, sir. I was afflicted by memories of the War and of my Vivien, brought on by the uncertainty and waiting. It was nothing more than that. You understand.'

'And yet you told me your employers had given you assurances, that there was no uncertainty. Weeks past you told me this: that your bank needed time to secure their position, order their affairs, but that they would pay your passage home, your expenses. Your rent.'

'Yes, of course.' Of course Tristram had said this, had

believed this would be so. No turning back, only to look straight ahead. Into the guns waiting on the other side, or into the bottom of her grave. 'I have not lied to you, mein Herr.'

'Then explain, please, young sir, the telegram in your pocket.'

No smile.

One hand sought out the other, fingers knotting.

He would say nothing, admit less. But light welled around the doorframe of that unoccupied room, the landlord and the hallway cast into silhouette before being consumed by the light as the door opened wider, light leaving only space enough for her to step from the room and come towards him.

Tristram could not turn away.

The hiss of her skirts was deafening.

Tristram pressed back against the wall.

She did not speak. The rustle of her long white dress was voice enough. He wanted to pretend, say it was mistake or misunderstanding. He would go straight ahead, through to the other side, and then he would be in his room again, lying on that narrow cot, waiting for tomorrow and the black sun's returning to watch him, post office and back, to lie on that narrow cot, in his room, waiting—

Her hands trailed shadows.

Amidst the light, Vivien's face was a blackness. Still, Tristram reached out, wanting to hold her again.

She passed between his arms, her white hands cool as they parted his jacket and let the fold of paper flutter to the hallway floor.

His landlord spoke. Tristram watched Vivien, shadows crossing her mouth, sculpting her face with a sweep of a delicate blade. Everything, in fact, he had imagined from her last letters.

'How long?'

His landlord repeated his question. Tristram looked

away. Through the window on to the narrow road tucked into Bárthori utca. Around this room, neat and orderly, unlike his own. Hard to believe his landlord lived here at all: always, it felt as though the apartment stood empty except for his infrequent visits, this interview, so neat, so tidy, so—

'How many more times?'

Tristram would have evaded that question, too, but the answer came: for as long as necessary. For as long as it took until there was someone willing to lend money, a...

He faltered over the word 'friend', imagining Villiers at the other end of the phone line. Villiers, his last resort. He found himself staring at his cardboard shoes. Seeing himself in the form master's office at school, gazing at the toes of his shoes as a way of weathering a reprimand. Drawing a breath, he straightened his shoulders, stood erect. Wanting to save some scrap of dignity.

His stomach grumbled loudly. There was no bringing himself to meet his landlord's gaze as, no longer kindly, the landlord read out the slip of paper again—the telegram that had finally arrived four days ago, its lines terse—stop—hopeless—stop—and final—stop.

'Was there never any hope? Your assurances, young sir, always worthless?'

He had almost left Budapest within days of last October's Stock Market Crash. But his employers had been quick to assure him there was no need. When the bank began to dissembled and draw out the time between each reply, Tristram had clung on to the belief that events would turn out for the good. Even as his employer's silence lengthened well beyond anything that allowed a benign explanation, he had held on to his belief. At least, a part of him had. It offered justification for everything he did that upheld that belief. Cheap lodgings. Pawning cufflinks, watch. Later, overcoat and suitcase and fountain pen. Finally his shoes. Each could be justified as easily as lying to his landlord to hold on to the room for one day more. Just in case. Because there was no saying when his employers might get in touch, when a friend might loan him what he needed, when… But all possibility had collapsed into this moment, a moment when there was no possibility at all.

Tristram felt the words, almost gave them voice. Instead, he sighed.

'I thought I was telling you something not entirely beyond the truth.'

His landlord remained silent, frayed cuffs and dirty spats lending him an odd dignity and a deeper sense of hurt. Tristram could summon nothing else to say and, little by little, allowed himself to become angry.

'What was I supposed to do? When the next day, or one after that, someone may have been willing to help? When there was still a chance the bank had not collapsed? No definite word, only doubt—'

'Be quiet,' his landlord murmured. Mild words as sharp as any blow, Tristram fell silent.

The telegram rustled. 'You have nothing?'

'Only what I'm wearing.'

Justification and belief. Tristram had tried to cling to the bank's own vision of itself—of an institution, small, oblivious to the ways of the world because it had its own way of doing business and those ways were older, more established and more sensible than everyone else's. Better hold on to a false dignity than have no dignity at all. Tristram's father had been much the same. Theirs was an old family, a proud family. It made no difference how little money they had. The family's dignity would see them through. And so Vivien had come into his life.

'I must have settlement.' His landlord folded the telegram—in half, into quarters—and tucked it into an inside pocket. 'This is intolerable. Simply intolerable, young sir.'

Tristram smoothed down his hair, touching at the stubble on his face (razor and hairbrush gone the way of suitcase, shoes and the rest) as his stomach groaned and knotted.

Dignity.

'Will it be the police, sir?' he asked, standing straight, shoulders back. At least being in custody should put a roof over his head, along with four stout walls and food. A future more certain than this.

'You are long past shame, my young sir?'

He thought of Vivien, of the final letter from her mother, its black border all the news he needed to hear. Another path closed.

'I...' The words were there but the energy to voice them was not. His shoulders slumped. 'Really, mein Herr,' Tristram shook his head, 'does it really matter?' He strode to the door. 'There is no sense in prolonging this.'

The handle would not turn nor the door budge.

'I have a proposition for you, young sir.' The landlord opened a bureau drawer, stirring its contents with a finger.

'Please, mein Herr.' Tristram rattled the door. It did not move, might indeed be fake, except he had come in through it earlier and times before that, too. 'I am content to speak to the police.' He felt hot, sweat making his grip on the handle uncertain. 'How—' He gave a hollow laugh. 'How does the door open?'

The landlord ignored the question and, instead, held out a hand. The locket lay in his palm. At first glance, it might have been ancient Egyptian, one of those cartouche pendants all the rage a few years back.

'This must be delivered to a particular jeweller before dusk today.' Large for a locket, resting in the landlord's palm. 'Take it.'

Tristram was going to decline but the locket was already in his hands.

The golden metal was badly scuffed and tarnished. Likewise the enamelling on its face was cracked, faded. Tristram could make out a bird—a pelican, perhaps—taking wing, a twig or something else in the creature's bill. Cheap gimcrack, he thought, locket springing open under his fingers, clasp faulty. The top hinged at either end, a portrait miniature slotted into the backs of the flaps, a man on one side, a woman on the other; faces marred and foxed, the vague impressions of their features as easily suggesting brother and sister as sweethearts, or a married couple. Tristram peered closer, finding no resemblance in either face to the landlord's features; sure, in one moment, these were paintings; convinced, in the next, they were photographs faded by light and time. Another enamelled image lay across the back of the case, the Sun's blazing visage dull, the Moon's profile no longer shimmering, each huddled on the clouded edges of the picture, unwilling to acknowledge the presence of the other. A figure stood between them, nude or swathed in classical robes: the damage to the enamel making it impossible to be sure, just as it made it hard to decide whether the figure was leaping, from Moon to Sun, or in some way trying to bring the two celestial bodies into contact, or balance. Or something else entirely—there was no telling, Tristram decided, assuming the spots on the figure's ankles were wings and guessing, then, the shape on its head was a winged helmet.

Mercury. No, Tristram thought, attention drawn again to the young woman, *Hermes*.

'Take this to be repaired and return, this evening, with the receipt, written in the jeweller's own hand.'

'If I do?' Tristram balance the locket on his palm, trying, for a moment longer, to pretend he had not already accepted the landlord's terms.

'If you do, then you keep your room and I see that you do not freeze, nor starve. I might even be able to help find money enough for you to return to your England. But—' the landlord raised a finger— 'do not think to fool me, young sir. I know the jeweller's handwriting exceedingly well.'

Tristram made no reply.

'You have less than five hours, young sir.' The landlord produced a slip of paper, the address written on it vaguely familiar. In any case, it would not prove difficult to find.

'Consider it done, mein Herr.'

The landlord made no reply and when Tristram tried the door, it opened with ease.

The sun wore old gold for its late afternoon appointments. Tristram walked to the end of Báthory utca, telling himself there was no need for haste.

A constable pointed down the long length of Andrássy út. And, confused by the throngs at the Oktogon, where the Grand Boulevard drives a chasm through the middle of Andrássy, one of the flower sellers was willing to peer at the fold of paper and point him southwards, a little to the west: *That way.*

Tristram, despite no specific idea of where the jeweller's shop lay, felt sure it could not be much further. Shadows welled in the streets and side roads; rooftops cut slices out of the dwindling sun. He checked the locket was safe, in the trouser pocket he had put it. And the address, still in his jacket pocket. Still safe.

Plenty of time, he reminded himself. And reassured himself locket and address were still with him. Trying to keep calm, because the landlord would wait until the utmost limits of his ridiculous deadline. Because panic might bring a mistake and a mistake might bring—

Plenty of time, Tristram repeated, wiping sweat from his face, air cooler with each step, the streets beginning to smell of a coming night. It was not far— Tristram looked at the address again, picturing a branch in the road, a row of old shops, memory more vague than it seemed right to acknowledge. Glancing at the sky, he told the sun another time that he knew the way, had nothing to worry about, nothing—

But in one doorway sat a woman whose legs were hardly stumps and whose hand, weather-worn, lay open and empty. And in another doorway, a man nodded over a rosary of his dreams, another casualty of time. And what of this man, on crutches, medal on his chest a Cyclops eye? Or this woman, this child, this—

Tristram broke into a run, locket prodding his thigh. He passed a beggar, white hair straggling from beneath a battered felt hat, eyes hidden behind smoked glass. The beggar turned, about to speak. Tristram ran harder. Just avoiding a match seller, scuffing along the line of the curb, tray filled with scraps no one would want. And a street singer, voice cracked and hopeless.

The locket pressed into his leg.

The newspaper seller looked over the slip of paper again, lips moving as he formed each word of the address. Tristram glanced at the sky, suppressed an urge to snatch back the address, to run, biting his lip until finally the newspaper seller handed back the paper and pointed along the street to the mouth of a narrow alleyway.

'That way.'

'There?' Tristram pointed, conscious of the weight of the locket against his thigh. 'There?'

'Yes.' The newspaper seller remained unbearably calm. 'Yes. To the end—' He waved his hand.

The first part of the alley was cobbled, each step painful thanks to thin cardboard soles and this race across Pest against the sun. Tristram tried to hobble faster, assuring himself it could not be much further and doubting each word as he repeated them to himself. Perhaps he could forge the jeweller's handwriting... Or, perhaps he could say the shop was closed, an emergency... Or, perhaps...

The passageway handed him into a lane of shops, men in shirtsleeves pushing laden handcarts between slow-moving motorcars and fast-moving children, shrieking as they ran. Confused, Tristram faltered, shying sideways as a football bounded towards him, a yell from one of the open shop doorways following close behind a child's laughter.

All in an instant, flinch and football and laughter and momentum picking one of his feet and making him step as, in this second's fraction already so packed, Tristram caught a glimpse of the limousine.

It gleamed, whitewall tyres riding over ruts and pothole with ease, bonnet pristine and more brilliant than any snowfield, sides and roof polished ebony, midnight dark as the chauffeur's livery...

Tristram saw the car, saw the driver, chauffeur's face quite undisturbed, as momentum picked up Tristram's foot and propelled him from flinch into step. Stumble taking him from pavement's edge into the limousine's path.

The lane reared back in shock.

Rooftops and doorways falling one over another.

No breath. Nothing. Not even pain.

The sky blinked. Stared down as Tristram blinked back. Heart stopped and breath forever stilled. The sky peered closer. Tristram stared at it, unblinking, his head filled with a din that reminded him of the last reverberation of an artillery barrage, or the silence in a room after sharp words and a sharp exit, he could not be sure which, although he tried to decide, certain that knowing was important. The low maunder of an engine went unnoticed, just as the reek of exhaust fumes, the taste of blood and the pain from bruises and strains went unnoticed. Until, explosively, Tristram gasped, drew a second breath that became a groan.

The black and white limousine stood a little way off. Afternoon light gleamed from its chrome. Spotless, unbloodied.

Tristram managed to sit, teeth gritted in expectation of a wave of pain that never crested. His tongue throbbed, bitten in his fall. A knee also complained, one wrist aching insistently, palms scraped and red but otherwise unharmed.

One of the curtains hiding the interior of the motor car twitched, revealing a face of alabaster perfection, a curl of ash blonde hair. All gone too quickly, curtain falling closed and the limousine gliding away. Around a bend in the lane. Gone.

It had been hours since the collision, or near miss—Tristram could not decide which—and yet people were only just leaving their doorways and businesses, only just beginning to cross the road towards him, voices raised, some shouting after the lost limousine, others simply standing back to watch.

Two attempts to stand.

Mumbling that he was fine, unhurt, quite fine, thank you, yes, thank you. A hand on his shoulder to steady him as he asked what time it was. Voices in Hungarian. In German. Tristram anxious the afternoon was lost and waving back all other attempts to help him. Assurances forgotten as he demanded the time, as his hand went to his pocket.

He checked again, more desperate this time, barking accusations to the people around him, their frowns transforming as they turned to looking across the road, in the gutter. The boy who had kicked the football apologised again, tears in his eyes, which Tristram ignored as he searched his pockets another time, finding only the address, useless now. He walked up and down, scouring the gutters, stopping every shopkeeper, passerby, demanding they look him in the eye, sure he would know lying when he saw it. No one had seen it. No one had taken it. It was lost.

The locket was gone.

He went to the jeweller's in any case, unable to shake the conviction that it would be waiting for him there, imagining the jeweller producing the repaired locket from beneath the counter, along with a signed receipt.

Shutters masked the shop's windows, only darkness nestled in the gaps between the dusty boards. It looked as though it had not been open that day, nor any day in recent memory. Tristram rattled the padlock and tugged on the bell pull. A chime sounded from deep within the old building but no one answered, no one offered to write a receipt for goods that had not been delivered.

The sun stole behind the hills of Buda and abandoned Tristram to the night.

It was difficult to find the way back to the small road tucked inside Báthori utca. At last, Dob utca appeared out of the night, willing to lead him part way before abandoning him when the opera house came into view, the crowds outside milling, faces redrawn by hard-edged electric light, jewels and cravat pins glittering, gaudy as the reek of cologne and perfume mixed with stale champagne and tobacco smoke, laughter singling him out, jostling, pushing until there was no choice but to hurry down a side road, taking another until the opera house was hidden. Tristram slumped against a wall, breath slowing. Nothing moved, the silence a relief and a comfort.

A soft whimper gently touched his hand, making him turn, mongrel dog poking its nose out of the lee of a doorway to eye him, length of string around the dog's neck leading Tristram to a cripple, asleep, crutch propped against the door. Homeless. Friendless but for the dog.

Tristram ran.

The entrance to the small road lay between numbers twenty-two and twenty-four, Báthori utca. He was almost at the crossroads with Hold utca before he accepted that he had missed the turning. Path retraced, he reeled out of the opposite end of Báthori, destination unaccountably overshot a second time.

And so once again, and with deliberation, Tristram counted off each tall building, unwilling to admit to the trembling of his hands, the sweat on his palms and forehead. Shadows hid the entrance, his hands expecting to meet mortar and brick, no matter that his eyes suggested the narrow passage was still open to the world.

But if the tall house waited as usual at the end of the small road, it acted as if it did not know him, no matter how loud he shouted, how hard he kicked the door. Its windows remained dark and blank, as closed off as the jeweller's had been. At last, Tristram remembered his latch key and laughed, at himself and at the once-kindly landlord. But the lock refused to recognise the key—old and tarnished as ever it had been, Tristram positive it had not been changed, yet the key would not turn.

Eventually, he had no choice; pausing to look back for what would be the last time, he left the small road.

The night felt colder. The curb stones spread a chill through his legs. Tristram shuddered, looking along the length of Báthori utca and unable to think of anything but the cold, the first glimmer of ice on the tarmac, new bruises aching more acutely. All of him seemed to ache. Tristram shook his head, sorrows trying to pull him from the edge of the curb to curl up in the gutter, as low as he could ever go. The cold poked at him until he yawned, icy air making his teeth ache, another sorrow, another sigh, sighs obscuring the sound of the engine, a purr moving through the streets nearby, entitled and confident and—as he sat very still—familiar.

A lamp's light drew a graceful arc over wheel arch, gleaming from a bonnet onyx white, whitewall tyres spinning hypnotist's passes at Tristram as he staggered to a halt in time to see the limousine shimmer over the crossroads with Hold utca, inciting him to run again, glimpse the car being swallowed by the elegant and ornate mass of the hotel dominating this stretch of Hold.

Hold utca. *Moon Street.*

Tristram looked up. Moon in first quarter, swelling with light.

A portcullis barred the entrance to the garage by the time he reached it. Blackness beyond. No sound. Tristram clung to the bars, too weak to stay upright without help.

'A handsome vehicle that, almost as pretty as its passenger. I take it you've witnessed the fair Alba for yourself, my friend?'

The restaurant was called A Varangyos Tó—The Toad Pond. It squatted on the corner of Széchenyi and Nádor utca, only a handful of streets away. 'My name is Voit,' was all the stranger offered, refusing any more until he had ushered Tristram to a corner table in the restaurant.

'Please, please,' Voit soothed as Tristram once again exclaimed over his new acquaintance's generosity. 'You are in distress. You must rest, dear sir, yes, rest. Sit, if you please, and gather your resources, I implore you. Do not—' Voit raised a finger, a pale and bony exclamation point— 'think you presume, dear sir. No, it is *I* who invite.'

Voit smiled. With his high forehead and pallid complexion, the effect was reminiscent of a death's head. Tristram's stomach rumbled, knotting about its emptiness. He put away his doubts and allowed himself to be convinced.

The food was as fine as it was welcome as it was plentiful. Soon, Tristram stopped apologising for being a poor conversationalist, apologising for his hunger, apologising for having apologised, and concentrated on the progression of entré to soup to main course, each overseen by Voit's smile and warm assurances that there was no reason to apologise, that Tristram's preoccupation was more articulate than any speech of gratitude and appreciation.

Tristram nodded. And ate another slice of goose.

After a time, he was able to sit back and sip wine, blood-rich and heady, and look around the dining room more or less for the first time. It was black: walls, floor tiles, ebony tables and even the upholstery on the chairs a deep shade that existed only long after midnight. Skulls were mounted on the walls—two stags, a lion, what could have been a wolf—bone startling against their backgrounds. Only the ceiling offered colour, although most of its expanse was a dusk grey that gathered the walls to make the room stand closer around the table than its true size would otherwise permit. A zodiac swept over the dining room, reigning over all, its twelve houses marked by their astrological sign and by the stars of their associated constellation in gold and silver, a compass rose of twelve points at the centre of the design, conducting the murmur of conversation around the gaslit room.

'I had no idea this place existed.' Tristram drained his glass.

'It is those things we walk past each day without noticing their existence that have the greatest power over us.' Voit paused to finish his own wine. 'Don't you find?'

He made the smallest gesture. A waiter materialised to refill their glasses.

'But, please—' Voit drank again— 'time for such things

later.' Voit turned his attention to his own plate, attacking his meal with enthusiasm and evident pleasure, pausing to await refill before drinking again and again. The wine sat uneasily on Tristram's stomach, food richer and more plentiful than he was accustomed to. But he was not about to offend this stranger's hospitality and, when a fresh bottle appeared, he nodded enthusiastically. The zodiac rose turned the conversation about them, a susurrus of Hungarian, of German, of French, other voices speaking in languages he could not recognise. He finished the last scrap of cabbage and drained his glass another time.

'Thank you,' he told his benefactor, trying not to slur. 'I can't begin to tell you—'

'Then, please, dear Tristram, do not attempt to. I see your expression and this is thanks enough.'

Tristram nodded. Noticed that there were three empty bottles of wine on the table, a deep dent already knocked out of a fourth. This bothered him, a little, but was not the thing that bothered him most. 'How...' He looked away from the bottles, their number a distraction from the question he was struggling to form. 'How is it you, do you know, my...'

'Your name? Oh, dear friend.' Voit laughed, patting Tristram's arm. 'Why you told me, remember? As we walked from hotel, the Ikrek. You remember? Of course you remember, of course you do, dear Tristram.'

'Oh.' Tristram nodded. Slowly. 'Yes. Silly of me.' *Ikrek*... meant... Tristram squinted at the table, the stem of Voit's glass melding from two into one. 'Ikrek' meant twins. Tristram glanced at the ceiling. *Gemini.*

'Dessert, I think, yes?' Voit smacked his lips. 'To sooth the digestion and aid the restoration of the body?'

Tristram tried find a polite way of declining, his stomach full and beginning to feel rebellious. But speaking seemed much too much effort, nodding so much easier. So he nodded and waved a hand. His wine glass tottered and moments passed while he rummaged for a causal connection between nodding and the glass's inability to remain upright. But it had been the wave of his hand, not the nod.

A waiter deftly caught the glass and placed it at the centre of the table before vanishing into the shadows.

'But, yes, on second thoughts...' As he spoke, Voit unbuttoned his double-breasted suit jacket and the waistcoat beneath. 'Upon reflection, my dear friend.' Voit patted his stomach before pressing his hands, palm to palm, fingertips brushing his chin. 'If I may venture a pause, a short rest, before we complete this delightful meal? Do you agree, my dear Tristram?' His new friend took out a tarnished silver cigarette case. 'Would you...?'

Tristram began to shake his head. The dinning room began to feel giddy and he was forced to mumble a no. Voit sat back and lit a long, thin cigarette rolled in deep brown liquorice paper as dark as the walls, the tables and floor itself.

Voit smiled through the smoke and drank more wine. The zodiac turned above them, the skulls unblinking.

The silence was companionable. Tristram found he was helping himself to more wine. Voit declined, his glass full for the present. Tristram tried not to stare at his new friend, wondering why and where and—

'Czech, kind Tristram. I am originally from that Bohemian city founded on the very hill where Lucifer, the bright Morning Star Himself, plummeted to earth upon His expulsion from the Christian Heaven. Praha. Prague,' Voit explained, patting Tristram's hand. Smiling, Voit instructed the waiter to forego desert and, instead, 'Bring out a bottle of that very fine Tokay I know is in your cellars.'

Tristram roused himself to argue. And thought it might sound churlish, after all.

Voit's smile grew wider and, between the shadows of gaslight and strong, blood red wine, that smile appeared as broad and fixed as any of the skulls mounted on the walls.

Tristram closed his eyes and willed his stomach to settle.

When a slim decanter of straw-gold arrived, the bouquet helped clear his head and the first sip was a warmth and a contentment that eclipsed the meal so far. The Tokay made him feel better than he had in many months. If not years.

'I am glad.' Voit smiled. 'It takes no insight to see that you have had a most trying time, my dear friend. We have broken bread and so are friends, firm friends, yes? And thus, now, if you would be so kind, I would hear a little of your story.'

Tristram searched for words, the events of the last months suddenly distant. He looked again at the slim decanter. It was nearly empty, as was the restaurant.

'Alas, your tale is most troubling.' Voit lit another of those thin, pungent cigarettes. 'To be stranded so—the distress is clear.'

Tristram thanked Voit for his understanding and sat back, unable to recall what he had said. One point suggested itself:

'The car, the black and white car… The young woman—a passenger, not the owner?'

'Indeed, very much the opposite, friend Tristram.' Voit sipped his Tokay and peered back over the top of his glass.

'Ah.' Tristram roused himself again a moment later to wonder: 'The owner, then, you know the owner?'

'I could not, in any form, describe myself as one his inner circle—if you take my meaning—but I know something *of* him, yes.' Voit drained his glass and a waiter appeared to replace the empty decanter with a full one. 'Nox. That is the name of the owner of the black and white limousine and of the fair Alba, also.' Voit leaned across the table, low voice filled with unusual passion. 'Attar Nox—a cold, harsh man who is notorious for taking a straight line through life's matters, regardless of what might lie in the path of that line.'

'Are you—' As Tristram reached for the Tokay, a waiter deftly slipped the decanter from under his hand and filled both glasses before retreating into The Toad Pond's black walls. 'Are you truly saying, Voit, that this Nox deliberately…?'

'Oh…' Voit sat back. 'I was not a witness, I could not be certain but…' He offered an eloquent shrug. 'It would not be out of his character.' He drank, swirled gold around his glass before drinking again. 'He employs gangsters. As bodyguards. Genuine American hoodlums. Nox's chief bodyguard—one Floyd, I believe—is reputed to have once been a 'torpedo' for Mr Al Capone himself.' Voit gave this a moment to sink in before continuing, 'There are many dark things said of Attar Nox so, based on his reputation, it might be no coincidence that your paths…'

Voit laughed and patted Tristram's hand.

'But you survived, my dear friend, be thankful for that.'

'I lost…' The murmur of the car's engine returned. It threatened, without becoming explicit. And he saw those whitewall tyres, the bodywork unmarred and gleaming. Disdainful as he had lain in the gutter.

'It would be a trifle to Nox. Not even that, I would say, his fortune is vast, you see.'

Behind the curtains, seated beside Alba, there might have been someone, in the shadows, watching… 'But who is he?' Tristram drained his glass. 'A bootlegger? A smuggler? Who is this, this—'

'Felon who came so close to running you over? This man who, without thought or contrition, dashed all your hopes?' Voit rose to his feet. 'Would you like to see the Beast, close at hand?'

Paintings of dancing couples slinked across the walls. The air was filled with the mingled scents of perfume and cigar smoke, liquor and a sweeter overtone that Tristram did not recognise but suspected might be hashish.

Voit was whispering with the nightclub's maître d'.

Tristram closed his eyes. The club's entrance lobby continued to sway in time to the music sashaying down the ornate staircase. He swatted the air, staggered but managed not to collide with the dancers on the wall.

'My friend,' Voit explained to the maître d', 'is suffering from an unfortunate infection of the inner ear. He will be so much happier once we are comfortably seated.' There was a rustling of money.

'I am perfectly well.' Tristram summoned what he imagined to be a confident and beneficent smile.

The maître d' raised an eyebrow a fraction but made no other comment as he instructed a waiter to take them upstairs.

Hot jazz and a gust of humid air greeted them as they stepped into the nightclub's main room. Aside from electric lights trained on the small bandstand, the room was lit primarily by candles on each table. Tristram rubbed his eyes, trying to clear his vision. The fog remained and he assured himself it was nothing more than smoke and shadow.

A cornet wailed. Champagne corks popped to the rattle of a cocktail shaker. Glasses clinked. A man's voice, deep and rough-edged, rising out of the gloom to roughhouse and jolly. People gyrating wildly on the scrap of dance floor in front of the bandstand. Half glimpsed shapes turning out to be more murals, paint gyrating wildly on the walls. A clarinet wailed. A woman tittered. Drum roll, cymbal crash. Heads bent back, mouths wide. Laughter and the rasp of a trombone... The chair beneath him was reassuringly solid. Voit made passes in front of the waiter's eyes and, an instant later, a cork rose free to let wine, rich and sanguine, gush into the glasses in front of them.

'Cocktails and whisky have their places but, for a night such as this...' Voit drained most of his goblet. 'And there he is: *voilà*!' Voit's swaying glass pointed, into the gloom beyond the nearest clutch of tables. Tristram opened his eyes wider. The smoke and the light made it hard to focus. A gout of shadow lay between the tables and the musicians shoulder to shoulder on the bandstand. Tristram leaned back in his chair, swaying as he tried to peer around the shadow towards what he assumed Voit was pointing to.

'No, no.' Voit heaved on his arm. The chair thumped back on to four legs. 'Look more closely,' Voit hissed loudly.

A waiter. Tray laden and held high, weaving between the close-packed tables. Waiter there and gone in the space of two steps, consumed by that gout of shadow.

Tristram knuckled his eyes. After a large mouthful of wine, he leaned forward, squinted through the roils of smoke until the shadows gained form and became tall, folding screens decorated with murals like those on the club's walls. What could be an elbow protruded. Possibly the back of a chair. And, puzzle rearranging itself, he saw the screens stood open towards the bandstand—a private booth in a public space.

The waiter stepped out from behind the enclosure, a tall, very heavy-set shape in a tuxedo following him to pause and survey the club, face revealed as hard and suspicious.

Another moment and the bodyguard was gone again behind the screen.

Voit's smile was wide, teeth long and white as he replenished their glasses, raised the wine bottle, the standard to which they were to rally, and lurched to his feet.

'We must approach. Oh, certainly yes, we must observe the Beast in his lair.'

He grabbed Tristram by the elbow and propelled them both across the room.

'But it was an accident,' Tristram protested, struggling to watch where he was going, avoid outflung arms, glasses and champagne bottles, and keep a look out in case the bodyguard reappeared. 'Nothing but a—'

'How can you be sure?' Voit turned abruptly. Tristram collided with his new friend, Voit saving him from falling into the lap of a drunken man before offering both Tristram and the man wine from the bottle. Tristram managed to miss his mouth on the first attempt, wine spatters down his shirt front appearing almost black under the club's lights. As he refilled the glass and guided it successfully to his friend's mouth, Voit expanded, 'Your landlord, did he not know of your most justified deception? And, knowing, could he not have instituted schemes and propositions most nefarious? Do you see the enormity of this plot?'

Both drained their glasses as they contemplated this insight.

'And thus,' Voit concluded, 'can there be certainty that news of your mission did not proceed the act of coercion that appeared to place you, so very randomly, on the corner of a particular lane at a particular time?'

'You mean...' Tristram frowned over thoughts reluctant to coalesce. 'My landlord?'

'Perhaps, perhaps, perhaps yes, perhaps no but rest assured, *someone* might have found out.' Voit nodded towards the folding screens.

'You're right.' Tristram was about to toast Voit but discovered his glass was empty. While Voit obliged, doubt had time to return. 'The locket was worthless, broken—'

'Broken, yes, but worthless...?' Voit's eyes grew wide. 'Was it not stolen? Without doubt it had value, for someone.' Voit threw his arm around Tristram's shoulder, hugging him close as he whispered, 'And, with *him*, there is a history of this.'

Voit's gaze managed to peer through the screens to the man seated behind them.

A muscle twitched in Tristram's face. 'The bastard—'

'Stealth, dear friend.' Voit held back Tristram's lunge. 'The bodyguards, a distraction. Yes,' he yelled, weaving towards the band, 'play that thing. Play something hot, hot, hot—' He reached the bandstand and waved high his wine bottle, taking a half-step sideways to ensure he blocked the view from within the screens.

'Play 'St Louis Blues'! Play 'Trouble in Mind'!' Voit swayed wildly, flinging his arms about. Wine spattered in several directions but mostly behind him, towards the screened table. 'No, no, no, I tell you what to play. Play 'That's-A-Plenty'!'

Tristram was paralysed. When two bodyguards emerged from the screened enclosure, he almost threw himself towards the bandstand in an effort to save his friend. At the last instant, he reached for the screen itself, almost toppling it over as he bounded around its edge.

A glimpse of two more bodyguards, stationed at the rear

of the enclosure. Forgotten as he met the gaze of the man seated at the table, a flash of consternation quickly masked behind elegance and privilege. There was a cruelness that was almost handsome, emphasised by the slashed line of his pencil moustache.

Nox. His tormentor. Without a doubt.

And beside him…

Tristram knew that he had at most seconds. Long enough to make an accusation, or unmask the conspiracy. But she was paler than his memory of her, framed in the limousine's window. Nox's eyes were a soulless black; hers winter sunlight on ice, startling but neither cold nor dismissive. And, as he rounded the screens' edge, she reared back in shock, yet there was grace still, a sense of fragility. There was something in her that reminded him of Vivien, his dreams of his fiancée haunted by this very mood of vulnerability and delicacy.

And so he saw Alba for the second time.

Hands slammed against his shoulders, grip heaving him backwards and off his feet. The motion finally freed his tongue.

'This man is a thief and a—' The collar tore on his jacket. A moment's freedom he used to sway back towards the table. 'A scoundrel. I know—' He waved a finger. 'I know—'

All four bodyguards grabbed hold of him. No time to wonder what might have happened to Voit. Two behind him pinned his arms while the two stationed at the table took hold of his lapels.

'I know,' he yelled. Accusing Nox. Trying to see Alba.

The band played more frenetically as he was frogmarched across the club, everyone pretending not to notice. Rather than open the door, they simply threw him against it, picking him up and throwing him a second time when the latch refused to budge.

If he was expecting to be booted downstairs and out the front entrance, his captors had other ideas, hustling him through a side door. A dingy set of back stairs waited for them to push and kick him from one landing to the next, across the hall at the bottom and out a door into an alley.

He quickly forgot any thought of fighting back. Better to curl up and hope the beating would end soon.

Tristram woke without memory of where he was. It was neither dark nor light, a frost biting against skin and bruise. Standing was impossible, so he crawled between broken furniture, crates of empty bottles and skitters of dog shit. A no-man's-land. Perhaps everything was an illusion and he was lost between the lines, memories of peace false, a torment meant to make his misery deeper and more complete.

His stomach clenched. There was nothing left to bring up. Tristram groaned, sniffed. Knew that no amount of crawling would help him escape the stink of vomit on his clothes. Better to hope for a fresh bombardment. Or a sniper.

'We are the Fallen, spirits imprisoned in mire.'

Vivien crawled alongside him.

'No.' He had to pause for breath, headache a spear between his eyes. 'Thirsty,' he told her.

'That's just the flesh,' Vivien replied.

She wore the same dress she had the last time he had seen her, the leave in 1918 just before he had gone back to the Front.

'The flesh rots on our bones and our souls,' Vivien reminded him. 'Stand or crawl, it's much the same.'

'No, you don't think that.' Another spasm clutched his stomach.

'Dearest,' Vivien sighed, 'you know full well the truth of the matter. Besides,' she continued as they crawled through a drift of peelings, 'that priest told you as much.'

He kicked open the vestry door, his men already sweeping the building, indignant curé standing in silence as the Maxim gun was deployed, as church became observation post. Tristram nodded to his subaltern and turned to the priest.

'*Mes sincères excuses, mon père.*' Tristram touched a respectful finger to the peak of his cap. 'I advise you to leave at once, sir. At once.'

But the curé stayed.

'This world of ours was not made by God.'

The words turned into ghosts, oil lantern turned low—to save kerosene, to offer as little light as possible to the watching night beyond the vestry's crudely blacked-out window—so the flame did nothing to blunt the chill. A fire would have been ideal, but the risk of the flames bringing attention had forced Tristram to veto any such thought.

'Then by whom, sir?' He shivered.

The curé sloshed more cognac into their cups. They had exhausted the last of Tristram's whisky the night before; the brandy might last till tomorrow.

'By the Adversary, Captain, by Ahriman.' The curé slurred his words. Tristram nodded politely.

'This is not the story in the Bible, *mon père.*'

'It is a truth hidden.' The curé offered more brandy. Tristram declined but indicated his host should go ahead, before asking him to explain further.

'Ahriman is a false god, a broken copy of the Ineffable, Captain, of the One, what you would call 'God'. When that entity— the true 'God', the One—withdrew to higher planes, Ahriman filled the void by creating the earth and the seas, the animals and the birds and the very trees they roost in. And, Captain, Ahriman created us. He made, as you can tell a poor job of it.'

Artillery sounded in the distance, bombardment set to continue for hours.

'Then—' Tristram put aside his cup— 'we are made in the image of… the Devil?'

'No.' The curé shook his head. 'Yes. In a sense. Ahriman is, perhaps, more Botched than Adversary, except as adversary to the Divine Spirit within us.'

'There is such?'

'Dim, guttering, near snuffed out in most, Captain.' The

curé saluted them both, drank, and refilled his cup. 'Nothing can exist that is not part of the Ineffable, even Ahriman. Even us. But the Divine within us is shackled to flesh made by an incompetent journeyman. We are what we are, Captain—inept copies of a Divine Plan that was guessed at, never actually witnessed. Ahriman forgets that the One exists, is convinced that Ahriman and Ahriman alone is God, and so believes the creations of Ahriman to be perfect beyond measure. Ahriman perpetuates each mistake and we, his crowning failure, are caught, generation after generation, in a hell of flesh and filth and decay.'

Tristram nodded, listening to the guns, crump of each detonation making the old church quiver.

'Is there no hope of salvation?'

The curé's silence was eloquent enough.

Vivien took Tristram's hand, tugging him from his seat in the vestry.

'I told you, beloved,' she whispered as she tripped him, pushed him back on to the alley floor, uniform becoming his old suit again, stained and ripped and reeking.

Tristram could not stop shivering. When he closed his eyes, he could still hear the guns, each impact flashing dimly, rumbling as it passed into silence.

Gears crunched.

His eyelids were crusted, unwilling to part. Tristram rubbed at his face until, blearily, he saw alley mouth and a little of the road beyond. A bowser rumbled past, spraying the gutters, spattering him with water. Tristram retreated, pulling scraps of cardboard and sacking about him for protection. After a little while, he slept.

He woke to find Voit sitting beside him. The day was grey and firmly overcast. Its light grated against the back of his skull.

'Cold.' The word hardly a croak. Those muscles not trembling were stiff and cramped.

'Alas, there is too often a morning after the night before.'

Voit sounded exhausted: suit jacket torn and stained, face pale beneath a greasy sheen, stubble growing in uneven patches and his hair dishevelled. Even the scent of cologne and liquorice cigarettes was gone, or become something more rank.

'They got you, too?' Tristram found he could not stop coughing, the urge to vomit again making tears run.

'I managed to make good my escape. In the end.' Teeth gritted, Voit heaved himself upright. 'Come.' Unsteady, Voit grappled with Tristram, both nearly collapsing before they managed to gain their feet.

Traffic criss-crossed in front the alley, passers-by noticing, now and then, these two tramps, and looking away.

After another minute, Voit coughed politely.

'I don't wish to remind you of your situation, but do you, by chance, have enough money for the bus?'

There was no point, but he went through the ritual of checking his empty pockets before admitting that, no, he did not have even the few coins needed for two bus tickets.

'Alas...' Voit turned out his pockets, upending his wallet, flapping its empty carcass once before dropping it to the roadside.

'They took your money?' A surge of indignation pushed aside the misery of hangover and thorough beating.

'I have nothing to show for the evening but your friendship, my dear Tristram.' Voit's shrug was philosophical. Cautioning only that, 'We have quite a way to go,' he began walking.

It was a district Tristram knew nothing of, sprouting from Baross utca, filled with tall, crumbling buildings and tiny, communal parks gone to ruin. Advertising hoardings proclaimed the luxurious flavour of this cigarette, the restorative effects of that brand of beer. Grubby shops collected many-eyed potatoes or bread that might have been more use replacing missing cobbles in the footpaths. Outside each shop, and on each corner, in caps or sagging felt hats, men loitered within clouds of cigarette and pipe smoke, their souls hidden behind blank, indifferent expressions. Gaudy tin signs hinted at the voluptuous delights to be enjoyed inside each bar; grimy windows and gloomy interiors suggested another story. And as the weeds straggling from broken curbs and sagging gutters were black with soot, so the air reeked of drains and chimney smoke and the canker of backyard foundries and chain works, their coal yards and the press shops that overlooked them, an abattoir with doors wide and runoff trickling into the gutter, to congeal, turn red to brown. To black.

Tristram found spit enough to swallow, a taste on his tongue that would not lessen.

But, turning another corner, Voit began to hum a snatch of Strauss and his dogged gait became almost jaunty.

'Home, be it ever so expedient,' he proclaimed.

A weathered nameplate proclaimed this to be *Holló átjáró*, Raven Passage, although it soon became obvious it was not any sort of passage: it led nowhere but skulked past derelict houses and shops, an occasional plot of vacant land boarded-up between, a high wall at the end bearing graffiti in countless different hands, including a fading raven, smeared over the brick in black paint or tar. It was beside this that Voit lived, in the floors above the remains of a shop, nameplate illegible under decades of grime, its windows missing behind battens and planks.

A reek of cabbage and cheap perfume met them in a cramped entrance lobby to show them up creaking stairs covered by a threadbare strip of carpet. A large communal room made a pretence of welcome, each of the doors leading off it firmly closed. Mismatched scraps of furniture littered most of the space, walls shrugging off their overcoats of ancient and nicotine-stained wallpaper.

A head appeared around one of the doors, stayed long enough to recognise Voit and provide Tristram with a glimpse of a mop of unkempt hair, chestnut dusting to iron grey, a female face, clipped and wan, before it vanished once again behind the door.

Without comment, Voit led Tristram up three further flights of stairs until they reached a low-ceilinged corridor at the very top of the building. Voit gave Tristram use of the room at the end; room enough, at least, to shuffle past the iron-framed bed, cold enough that it might have been open to the sky.

'Kitchen's on the first floor, toilet out back,' Voit yawned. 'Sleep as long as you care. I'm sure I shall.'

The bed gave rheumatic complaints as Tristram dropped on to it. He was desperately thirsty and no less in need of toilet facilities. An image of stairs and the vast distances contained within the house robbed him of energy. Promising to get up in a minute, he slumped across the bed. In moments, despair gave way to sleep.

It was a brothel, of a sort.

The woman he had seen was one of ten living in the house. The oldest might have been sixty or no more than thirty-five; the youngest wore an expression he recognised too well from the trenches—too much, too quickly, cynicism turning to fatalism.

Mostly, the women slept through the days, made desultory attempts at laundry or cooking, just enough to keep functioning. One or two went out in the early afternoon on the off-chance a factory worker or bar patron might be interested in more than food and beer for their midday break. Generally, they only came alive at night, once in a while bringing their work home with them. The noises carried to Tristram's room, where they offered another reminder of the war—of soldiers desperate for some kind of distraction, and of the sense of futility that had grown in him, become acute after his release from hospital and return to active service.

He touched the scar on his forehead.

The women of the house largely acted as if he did not exist and it was difficult to shake off the notion he was nothing but an observer, or a passenger, carried along by events, left with no choice but to adapt, to accept.

Voit was unconcerned.

'One must make a living, dearest Tristram, no matter how meagre.'

Voit acted as the women's procurer, sometime guardian, and landlord. They handed over all they earned, Voit pooling the takings and, in effect, keeping the women on a wage. Tristram could not decide whether the wage was fair or not, could not fathom how much Voit was skimming off the collective pot, although he was positive his friend took a bigger payout than anyone else. Whether the house was Voit's or whether, somewhere, there was a landlord, never became apparent, any more than the source of the affluence displayed on their first meeting; Tristram was left to guess at a gambling windfall as the source of meal and wine and, even, Voit's well-cut suit—his friend's clothes generally seemed much less splendid, although he tried to maintain an air of the dapper about him. But Voit's friendship and generosity was unchanged: there was never a hint that Tristram should pay rent, nor that he should assist Voit in his activities as the women's ponce.

'You have lost much, while I hold on to a little,' Voit said once.

Tristram was grateful, far more than he was able to show. Yet the house made him uncomfortable; a restlessness drove him out into the webwork of streets hereabouts, to watch and be watched: old women smoking clay pipes as they sat on the front step; children tottering back and forth under the weight of lunch pails or sacks of flour; money exchanged, furtive and swift, notes and coins no more than shadows evaporating whenever the sun pried through the soot-stained sky; a street hawker, a white cane guiding her between pocks in the footway, tray around her neck offering meagre pickings: a few bootlaces, a box of flints for a petrol lighter, Tristram stepping out of her way and the blind woman turning towards him, mouth opening although whatever she might have thought to say remained unsaid.

The house, dank at the best of times, grew steadily colder and damper with a change in the weather. No one complained, although the mood became more sullen. One afternoon, as the women were picking over food or laundry or dressing to go out, Voit appeared in the living room, announced there was no need for glumness, things were not so bad. Things, he proclaimed grandly, would be better come spring, when business was sure to pick up.

The speech made no dent on the mood, nor did anything to warm the house. The women either shrugged or ignored him. Tristram felt he should say something in support of his friend, but even Voit was retreating to his room, rousing speech forgotten.

There was a tug on Tristram's sleeve. It was the woman he had seen on first entering the house. She tilted her head towards the stairs, pulled his sleeve again. It took him a moment to understand she want help with something.

Her name was Sára. This much he got as they walked along Raven Passage, otherwise she said very little, even when they reached one of the vacant plots and she began loosening the fence boards.

'What are you doing?' he asked again.

'Waiting for you to lend a hand… *Uram* Tristram,' Sára added with a grunt.

Uram: 'mister', in common usage. With her tone of voice, he guessed she meant it more literally, more sarcastically: 'Lord'.

Tristram yanked one of the boards loose and together they widened the gap so they both could crawl through.

'We're looking for firewood, I take it?' he blurted as the boards thumped back in place behind them.

'What?' Sára peered back at him over her shoulder. 'Do you want to fuck?'

'No,' Tristram stammered. 'That's to say, I would, I mean—'

She tutted, face sour. 'Stop that. I don't want to fuck you, it's too cold. 'Sides, I bet you're like Voit.'

'Eh?'

Sára held up her little finger, curled and drooping. 'Can't get it up, he can't.' She snorted. 'Better that way. It's rubbish having a ponce who thinks he can jump on his girls whenever he's pissed enough to be randy. Bastards.'

She kicked a path through weeds and rubble as she spoke, stopping to turn back to where Tristram stood, mouth sagging a little, his face beginning to flush.

'Have I shocked you, your Lordship?'

Mockery and aggression, they were easy to see and hear, and it was these he responded too, blustering a little to cover his discomfiture as he hurried to catch up, brusque and, yes, a little lordly as they tramped through the overgrowth, wanting very much to regain some scrap of superiority. But when Sára tripped over a bramble, he resisted the urge to let her pick herself up unaided. And, when his foot dropped through a hole where an underground culvert had caved in, she grabbed his arm and gave him support as he clambered back to level ground.

At the far corner of the plot, the fence bordered the rear yard of one of the empty buildings.

'Found this last summer.' Sára stood back to let Tristram crawl between loosened boards first. 'Thought it might come in handy.'

He expected an old wood-store, open to the elements and so, in someway, fair game, like picking up windfall. But when she made him squint through a grime-crusted window, piles of furniture in a back parlour failed to quite block sight of an open doorway, hints of more rooms beyond. Sára rattled the locked back door and stood back, waiting.

'This is breaking and entering.'

She made no comment, simply waited.

'Theft,' Tristram clarified.

Sára opened her eyes a fraction: *Yes... so?*

'It's someone else's.'

'You'd rather be cold? Hungry? You'll do nothing, just accept an empty stomach and catch yourself a chill? Hm?'

He had no answer, no matter how much he cast about for one.

'An excuse then?' Sára jerked a thumb at the scene beyond the grimy glass. 'Nothing's moved in there this last six-month. Or, they've forgotten about it. The owner's dead. The furniture's stolen in the first place. The house—'

Tristram threw his weight at the door, ignoring the pain in his shoulder and barging against the wood until the frame cracked and the lock mechanism became loose.

There were enough scraps, worm-eaten and ancient, to keep them warm for several days without breaking down any of the larger pieces. As he piled up firewood, bundled it in with twine and bits of rope filched from the mildewed kitchen, Tristram speculated about the house, its owners—the still atmosphere of the place, the dust unmarred until they trampled across it, the deep gloom cast by the shuttered and boarded front windows—anything but question too closely what he was doing.

A sound from overhead startled him.

He could not climb the stairs, at first. Only when the sounds came again and he noticed that Sára had gone. She looked up from the drawer she was rifling when he at last found the room she was in.

'What d'you think?' She held up a cameo.

Unconsciously, he touched his pocket, a faint hope the locket might be there after all still lingering.

'Looks... cheap. Ghastly.'

Sára dropped the cameo on to a handkerchief alongside other knick-knacks and gimcrack. 'It'll make a little, anyway.' She glanced up, catching the look of discomfort just before it vanished from his face. 'Your Lordship?'

But there was no sarcasm in the title and she helped lug firewood outside and secure the backdoor against return visits without further comment, the two of them dragging the bundles back along Raven Passage. Tristram was sure they would be stopped at any moment, expecting a chorus police whistles. He pictured himself dressed in striped jersey and black domino mask, a sack labelled SWAG slung over his shoulder. But the passage remained deserted; even the magpies and crows took no notice of them.

'You can manage?'

He glanced at the remaining bundles waiting to be carried around the back of the house. 'Of course.' Expecting her to go inside, Sára started up the lane once more. 'Where—?'

She patted the bulge under her clothes where she had tucked the handkerchief of jewellery and gimcrack.

He nodded and, after wishing her good luck, kept his peace.

A gentle knock woke him from a shallow, troubled sleep. Heavy limbed, Tristram swung off his cot and tugged open the door. The hallway was empty, stairs creaking and footfalls descending to the floor below. Waiting on the threshold, a bowl of goulash, steaming. A chunk of black bread acted as paperweight, the note beneath in pencil, letters large, unsteady and diligently copied from a child's primer.

Pawnbroker said this was crap not ghastly.
Souvenir, your Lordship
Eat.

The cameo dropped to the floor.

'Of course you're an honest person,' Voit assured him. 'We are all of us honest people.'

'But—'

'Did not that great sage, the mystical Swedenborg, encourage us to do the good we can do?' Voit warmed his hands, rubbing palm against palm. 'And so we follow the great man's dictum, dearest Tristram. According to means and circumstance.'

Tristram wanted to say *But* again. Instead, he held out his hands and let the roaring fire warm him.

The house fell silent in the evenings with the last slam of the front door. Embers billowed, Tristram watching the last chunk of wood fall in on itself, flames dwindling, crackle to murmur.

You're more than welcome to join me, dear Tristram.

A bar, several streets away, a broad corner within easy reach. Voit's shopfront.

Perhaps some other evening.

As you wish, my friend, as you wish…

Almost a fortnight since then. Cuts healed, bruises fading. Cold slithered close to the chair as Tristram watched the fire gutter and cool. Each evening, he waited for the cinders to turn black and the chill in the communal sitting room to grow uncomfortable before climbing to his cot in the attic, to lie and watch the little smudge of sky visible through the grubby skylight. Some nights he heard Voit's return; more often Tristram fell into a sleep that was not entirely dreamless, images phantoms that waned with the coming of another day.

The embers in the fireplace began to creak as the heat left them. Soon, the only sound was his own breathing.

Tristram stared at the door to the stairs.

'Tristram, my dear friend.' Voit half rose and indicated the rickety seat next to his. 'Wine?'

Not waiting for a reply, Voit gestured to the barman.

The bar smelt of tobacco, pickling vinegar and paprika on the verge of turning rancid. A huge iron stove squatted in one corner, a baleful demon, smouldering and unapproachable; a broad fireplace stood across the room, cackling to itself and pretending not to recognise the existence of the stove. Voit ran his business from the lee of the fireplace, glass of red wine somewhere near to hand, a beneficent smile on his face as, periodically, he orbited the room, mooching through the ash trays for dog-ends.

'My second home,' Voit sighed, shredding cigarette stubs into his tobacco pouch. 'Be it ever so frowsy.'

Tristram sniffed the wine, wanting to believe there was more grape than vinegar in the glass. He pulled a face and, when courage allowed, swallowed the first mouthful. 'It grows on one,' Voit observed, advising a second mouthful to chase away the taste of the first.

Old men hid behind white moustaches, nodding beside the stove or pushing cards back and forth for matchsticks. Younger men peered at the day's newspaper or talked, voices growing louder in proportion to the quantity of beer or wine or rotgut pálinka they consumed. Now and then, one of them would wipe his mouth, stand and sidle across the room to whisper to Voit. Or a customer would come in off the street, walk straight up to the table beside the fireplace, or loiter at the bar awhile. Always the same hushed conversation, conducted as much in gesture and wink as in words. The deal might fall through. More often, Voit took money with the speed and grace of a pickpocket, praising his clients for making such a wise and pleasurable investment. Depending, Voit might call one of the women over from the corner across the street where they walked up and down and up, and Margita or Fanni, say, might disappear, arm-in-arm, with their latest client. Or, perhaps, Terézia or Agota were warming themselves by the stove, a glass of gin or a plate of stew half-finished when Voit called them back to work.

The nights passed, slow or quick, but they passed and Tristram found himself sleeping later, rising when he heard Sára moving around on the floor below, or when Voit shouted up the stairs that breakfast, humble and lukewarm as it was, awaited. After the door slammed each evening, Tristram banked the fire and waited, knowing it was a game, lingering in any case—as if, this evening, he might stay in all night, listening until the silence grew heavy, until the house felt too still, too empty—before slamming the door behind him and walking to the bar.

This night: raised voices ahead. Recognising Dorottya's voice, the man's unfamiliar although his intonation was clear enough.

'We're not—' Tristram stepped smartly around the corner, the man startling— 'a charity. And we don't,' Tristram emphasised, 'offer anything for free.'

'Fuck off.' The man recovered and puffed out his chest.

'Pardon me?' Before the man had time to react, Tristram took a swift step, feet almost crushing the man's toes, close enough the reek of sweat and beer almost made him flinch. But Tristram showed no reaction, leaning closer as he repeated, 'Pardon me?'

'Er...' The man looked at the pavement. Or the nearest wall. Anywhere but at Tristram. 'She's too fat, anyway,' he finally shouted, running away.

Two deep breaths before Tristram could speak. 'Would you like to come into the bar for a few minutes?' He had no idea how he managed to keep a tremor out of his voice. He turned to Dorottya. 'A glass of wine?'

'I'm fine, *Uram* Tristram.' She pulled her shawl a little tighter across her skinny shoulders and sauntered off. 'Thanks,' she called over her shoulder.

Tristram slumped down beside Voit. When he felt Voit studying him, he tried to hide the disgruntled expression, although the set of his shoulders alone must have spoken volumes. Voit made no comment but signalled the barman.

A small brandy appeared on the table.

Voit pretended to be concentrating on shredding dog-ends when Tristram finally moved, glancing from brandy glass to his friend and back, the first sip almost stripping the flesh from his throat, the second little improvement, although the alcohol was beginning to have effect by then.

Half an hour later, Dorottya came into the bar, exchanged a joke with the card players and came over to Voit, dumping a handful of coins on the table in front of him.

'Ah, thank you, most kind and sensuous lady.' He picked tobacco from his tongue, balancing his cigarette on the edge of the table ahead of counting this addition to the night's takings. Dorottya leaned forward, trapping several coins under bony fingertips and sliding them across the table to

Tristram.

Voit watched with no more comment than a raised eyebrow.

Tristram, no less speechless, looked from coins to woman. Dorottya curtseyed before bursting out into a cackle, its sound somehow loitering in the bar even after she strolled out.

Sára could not stop laughing.

'It was a surprise.'

'She said the look on your face—'

'It came as an utter surprise.' He could hear a haughtiness in his voice, face becoming flushed. He paused in front of a fruit and veg stall, pretending interest in chestnuts and quince.

'She was grateful.'

'She has an odd way of showing it,' he sniffed, picking up an apple and setting it aside.

'Really, your Lordship, you don't want the money?'

He drew breath. Rather than speak, he turned away from the stall, striding along the street.

'Your Lordship?' Sára matched his stride and he wanted to tell her to leave him alone, that he had no wish to be seen with such a person.

'It's—' Tristram halted, hands raised and fingers spread, trying to squeeze sense from the cold, dull air, clouds heavy this afternoon, squeezing the light out of the city. 'It's… immoral. They're immoral earnings, aren't they?' And, this time when he looked to her, pretence was gone. 'Aren't they?'

'Money's money.' Sára shrugged. 'Doesn't matter where it comes from. Just that you have it. Or that you can do without it.' Another shrug and she bit into an apple.

'Did you—?'

She would not come back with him. But he took the apple from her. The stall keeper hardly listened to the story about mistakes and distraction. 'I'll take this one, too.' Tristram handed the greengrocer one of the coins Dorottya had given him and returned to Sára. He handed both apples to her.

Sára held out the uneaten apple 'Thank you, *Uram* Tristram.'

At last, he took the apple and bit into it.

He said nothing

He did not go back to Raven Passage but walked, taste of the apple lingering. He bought a cup of tea at a little café beside the theatre on Jókia square, faces on the lobby cards and posters watching him.

The taste of the apple lingered.

Soon, the afternoon sapped the warmth from the tea and there was no choice but to walk faster as he crossed the boulevard and turned along Báthory utca, numbers twenty-two and twenty-four already behind him before he thought to look for the entrance to the small road where he had once lived. A voice called out, his name. Tristram glanced, stopping to turn and look, but the footpath was deserted, as was the length of Báthory utca.

He stopped outside the chemist's shop on the corner, a guilty pang trying to convince him that someone in the house on Raven Passage would be missing him, that Voit might be concerned.

From this angle, the Hotel Ikrek was little more than a shape amongst the trees lining that section of Hold utca. He could not expect to see any more than this, it was preposterous. The afternoon pressed closer, face grey and the tang of apple sharp on its breath.

Tristram started walking.

Night came blustery and sharp-tongued, rain tapping at one window of the bar, getting bored and coming around to pelt the other side. The paprikash had finally succumbed to old age and the barman was busy tying to scour the worst sludge from the bottom of the pan, the bar almost deserted but for the card players, who dealt each new hand more slowly than the last. The women of Raven Passage took turns to patrol outside; otherwise, they sat around the stove, sullen, listless, the level in their glasses of gin hardly moving, hour on hour.

Tristram found himself telling Voit about the curé and Ahriman. That led to the vision, in the alleyway behind the nightclub, and to Vivien.

Voit nodded from time to time, attentive as he rolled another ragged cigarette, tongue darting along the seam in the liquorice paper.

'Your priest sounds a wise man, Tristram.' Voit struck a match and inhaled. 'He still lives?'

Tristram shook his head.

'Pity.'

Glasses appeared and spirits, colourless as water but no more pure than sin, sloshed, spattering the table. The barman mumbled something about it being a foul night, too distracted by some great sorrow to accept their thanks.

'You have not mentioned a fiancée before, friend Tristram.'

Tristram sipped, grimaced, sipped again. 'No.'

'Ah.' Voit drew sharply on his fag, smoke coiling around his long, spare face. 'Should I infer an estrangement?'

Next sip a hot coal trapped at the base of his throat. 'Yes.'

'And she is beautiful, this Vivien of yours?'

'Very. Almost perfect, one might say. Dark. Raven-dark hair and eyes, a deep brown that could appear black, and skin pale and pure—like marble, Voit, but not hard, not cold, you must understand that, no matter that she might seem carved and hard, not Vivien, Voit, do you see?'

'Of course, my friend.'

'Overwhelming. She could be overwhelming.' Tristram turned his glass round and around on its base.

'You were engaged long?' Voit asked.

'We were engaged two years before the war.'

'But you have severed ties with her? A result of your

exile here? No, surely not.'

'No. We parted after the war ended.' Tristram drained his glass, almost choking on the rough spirits.

'I am saddened, dear Tristram, the lady Vivien clearly means much to you.' Voit offered Tristram a cigarette. 'No?' Voit snapped the lid back on the tin. 'There is no possibility of reconciliation, even after all this time? If you were to go to the lady Vivien— Where is she?'

'Wales. She's at her home in Wales. And there's no chance of reconciliation, even after all this time, Voit, no. But thank you.'

'For?'

'Listening.'

Voit waved a hand. 'Do not mention it. Even if the evening were more stimulating, I should be delighted to listen, my dear friend.'

'If you'll excuse me, Voit.' Tristram stood, carefully placing his chair under the table. 'I shall turn in for the night.'

Voit made salaams and wishes for pleasant dreams.

Sára looked up as Tristram opened the door. If she had been about to speak, he did not wait to find out but pulled the door firmly shut behind him and began walking, unsure of what direction to take, in spite of his excuses.

Footsteps. A voice snatched away by the wind. Hand on his arm not enough to make him stop straight away.

'Hey, Lordship, hold on.' Sára's face was hard to make out in the shadows between two street lamps. 'It's a slow evening. And you look glum.'

'Yes?'

'So I was wondering if you fancy that fuck we talked about? On the house—'

He very nearly struck her, fist aching and the urge to lash out blinding and revolting.

Sára startled back a step. 'Sorry—'

'No.' He drew another breath, deeper and slower than the last, made himself relax, made himself lower his voice and smooth the hard edge from it. 'No. I'm sorry. It's not you—'

He reached out for her and thought better of it. 'It's— It's—'
Bile rose in the base of his throat and the cold made the
shivering worse. 'I'm promised to someone. My fiancée. I
can't, I couldn't—'

'She'll never know, Tristram.' She began to reach out and
thought better of it. 'She won't—'

'But I'll know, Sára.' He spun, began to walk. 'Sorry.
Please.' Broke into a run.

The dawn came to sit on the curb beside him. It shivered and
fretted. Coins jangled in his pocket when he stood and the
urge to drop them, one by one, down the nearest drain,
clutched at his hand, tugging. The dawn, sleepless and grey
under the eyes, walked beside him when he crossed Andrássy,
wound a path towards the high dome of the basilica dedicated
to Saint István, agreeing they had no purpose nor end, simply
to walk, keep walking until, at last, he stood under the trees
again, a thin mist clinging to the ornate roof, floor on floor of
windows mostly unlit, the hour still early, the dawn keeping
watch beside him until the hotel doorman noticed and came
out to stand and glower until Tristram trudged up Hold utca
towards Báthory, the dawn already long gone, delivery lorries
nosing into the service road alongside the hotel.

He slept for a few hours in the cot in the attic room, dreams
of Vivien coming and going, seeing her as she had been on
their last meeting, walking along the seafront at Aberystwyth,
winds driving each wave far up the shingle beach, tugging her
hair, hair streaming, so pale it might well have been ash.

'Sorry.' He placed the present on the table in front of her. 'I
hope there are no hard feelings.'

She sniffed, shrugged, carried on with her mending.

He turned to go back to his room.

'Did you buy this with immoral earnings? I couldn't ever

touch it if you have.'

'I stole it,' he told her, not turning around.

'Oh, that's alright then, your Lordship.'

After a moment, he heard her take a bite out of the apple, chomping loudly as she began sewing again.

'Tell me about this Nox.'

Voit drew on his cigarette. 'Attar Nox... Let me see...' He dabbed the end of the fag in an ashtray, careful not to crush it so he could pick out the unburned tobacco. 'An Armenian by birth, it is said. And, also it is said he is originally Georgian. Consensus says our fellow hails from Black Sea. Or, possibly a little further westward.'

Voit looked up hopefully as the door opened but it was one of the card players, shaking rain from his coat. Voit subsided.

'There is no consensus,' Tristram suggested.

'Quite.' Voit signalled the barman, who appeared more morose than usual. Red wine sloshed itself into their empty glasses.

'You know him, though?' Tristram prompted, grimacing at the acid wine. 'You know his wife, at least.'

'My dear friend,' Voit protested, '*of*—I know *of* this man's wife as I know *of* this man. Do you see?'

'Yes, of course—'

'I am aware, dearest Tristram, of the myth and the story of our dear and absent nemesis, Herr Nox.'

'Nemesis?'

'A rhetorical device on my part, my good and dear friend. And yet...' Voit paused, considering. 'You still hold to the theory that Nox took your locket?'

'I never said— you—'

'But you think it might be so, yes? Hence this line of questions? Hm?'

'I suppose.' Tristram looked across the room, to the group of women around the stove, the card players, the barman leaning on the bar, chin on his fist. 'I'm curious about Nox. And Alba. In so far as—'

'Everything pertains, when it comes to Attar Nox.' Voit sipped wine and began.

There were several competing tales—one that Nox was the illegitimate son of royalty, another that he had in fact begun his career as a sailor and smuggler, of opium or guns or people, whatever might bring the highest return at any one time—but it did seem likely that he had somehow become adopted by a wealthy family while still a young boy.

'He became a usurper, manoeuvring the rightful heir aside. Patricide,' Voit hissed. 'In a sense,' he continued in more normal tones, 'it not being his blood father he killed. In any event, he gained himself a fortune and used that to accrue even larger rewards. Nox has most certainly travelled the world and most certainly been peripheral to numerous activities of an unsavoury but lucrative kind. Never enough for the paladins of the law to take collective action and, in those instances where a detective or similar has taken the initiative alone, said detective or similar has come to leave law enforcement, in some fashion or another.'

He sipped his wine.

'Ruthless. Single-minded and ruthless, these are the qualities of our adversary. The beautiful Alba is his prisoner.' Voit's hand twitched, spilling wine. 'What a shameful waste,' he observed. 'In any event, he treats her as ornament and centrepiece, carrying her around with him wherever he travels, never allowing her to stray far without him.'

A trio of possible customers stumbled into the bar. They descended on the group of women beside the stove in the fashion of myopic vultures. Voit sighed, waving Tristram back into his seat, sure these patrons would cause no trouble. Money changed hands. Margita laughed at a slurred joke from one of the newcomers, her performance almost worthy of an award, Sára shot a long-suffering look towards Tristram as she linked arms with another of the men and began to laugh so heartily one could almost be convinced the thing her life had lacked up to now was a funny joke.

Éva making up the party, they rolled out through a side door, corridor beyond leading to stairs, rooms several floors above.

'It is said she was the daughter of nobility.'

'Alba?'

Voit sat beside the fire again. 'A distant relation, betrothed to a very fine young man whose only misfortune was to be seen as a rival by Nox. You will not be surprised to hear the fate of Alba's betrothed was catastrophic.'

Voit swallowed the last of his wine and grimaced.

They changed the subject after that, or the subject changed itself. But the words wandered alongside Tristram, the next day and the morning after that and for days to follow, as they dawdled across town, never with any purpose consciously in mind other than, at a stretch, to revisit old haunts. And so, Tristram turned over the words, a syllable at a time as he stood, again and again, under the trees, looking upwards at floor upon floor of windows, any one of which might have someone looking out at the street below.

On another night, Tristram placed a packet of Turkish cigarettes on the table before Voit.

'I shall say only thank you, dearest Tristram—' Voit deftly opened the packet— 'and hope this most keenly appreciated gift put you to no inconvenience.'

'None in the least.' Sára had persuaded him to help her break into another house, less neglected than the first but almost as abandoned. They had gathered candlesticks, and other swag portable and easily moved on, into a pair of pillowcases. When he had declined a share of the proceeds, Sára had pressed coins into his hand and told him to buy himself a drink or a packet of fags.

'Then I doubly thank—'

The scream froze them. The yell of anger released them.

They burst into the street. Saw Kata trying to wrench the lid off a dustbin. Saw Agota struggling with a man, fist pulled back ready to land another punch on the side of his face.

Tristram sprang forward. There was a flash, an instant of recognition as the flush of fear reminded him of the moment after the whistles blew, swarming up the ladders into no-man's-land.

The dustbin lid came free with a clang.

Agota swung wildly, fist striking with a dull slap against the man's eye, man roaring, swearing all the more, one of his hands rising, too late to ward off the blow but hitting Agota across the mouth, drawing a gout of blood as she fell back, swearing herself.

Tristram took hold of the man by the neck, momentum spinning them both, pulling them apart to dump the man into the gutter and pitch Tristram into the nearest wall.

Kata screeched a threat, swinging the dustbin lid. It hit the curb, narrowly missing the sprawling man's head, a blow that might have killed him. He rolled aside, spitting and swearing.

'All fat, the lot of you. Like pigs in lard. Fat.'

'You?' Tristram was too surprised to react.

The man who had argued over paying Dorottya spat at Tristram, scrambling until his feet were under him and he could begin to run.

Tristram knew he should just let the man go. Something, instead, propelled him from the wall, shooting out a leg, kicking the man in the thigh. The man dropped, squealing as Tristram closed in, ready to deliver another kick.

The rush caught him by surprise. The man up, swearing and punching, hurling himself at Tristram, most of the blows missing, but the force of the attack enough for Tristram to overbalance, fall.

'Fuckin' show you, fat bastard, you fat fuckin' fucker, I'll show the fuckin' lot of you—' A litany of grievances, each punctuated by a blow. Tristram fended off the first few, dimly aware of Agota's screams, part pain, part affront, mostly fear and rage, and the scrape of the dustbin lid, imagining Kata snatching it from the road. 'Show fuckin' show fuckin' show you fuckers—' The punches fell harder, endless. Tristram managed one blow, two, but the man kicked and punched harder. It was difficult to breath or think. If he could simply make enough space between them to drive a kick—

'Fuck off now, thank you so much.'

Voit calmly cuffed the man across the shoulders with the dustbin lid another time. The man cowered, swore, tried to fight back and got the dustbin lid in the arm.

'Yes, kindly fuck off, there's a fellow.'

Agota dabbed blood and spittle from her face, shrilling that she hoped his prick continued to shrink, which would serve him right for making her bite her lip so. She spat at him. Kata, rubbing her bruises, spat too before telling him to piss off.

'I'll fuckin'—'

'What?' Voit asked reasonably, gesturing with the dustbin lid. 'Do fuck off.'

Voit helped Tristram to his feet. Kata already had her arm around Agota's shoulders, drawing the other woman in the direction of the bar.

'I'll get you next time.' The man backed further away. 'You fuckin' little fucker, I'll fuckin' get you.' He pointed at Tristram.

With space to breathe and think, Tristram simply flicked two fingers in his direction.

'I'll remember you, you fuckin'—'

Tristram snatched the dustbin lid from Voit, pulling it back to hurl, a giant discus aimed at the man's gut.

The man turned and ran up a side road, slap of each footfall soon lost to the night.

'I feel like a fool.'

Hands trembling, heart refusing to slow. Sweat oozed, soaking him through and leaving him cold despite the fire in the grate, the huge stove smouldering balefully on the other side of the room. The card players had abandoned their game to watch the altercation and its aftermath, the women clustered closely around Agota and Kata.

'Nonsense, sweet Tristram. You won the joust.'

'I made a bloody fool of myself.'

'I disagree. You stepped in where others would not.' Voit lifted his wine glass in a toast. 'I salute your courage, dearest friend.'

'I don't think—'

'Don't whine so, *Uram* Tristram.' Sára placed a glass of oily, colourless spirits in front of him. 'Pálinka,' she explained. 'We clubbed together. Drink.' She nudged the glass closer.

His hands trembled too much to lift the glass without spilling most of it. Anchoring it on the table, there was no choice but to lean down and slurp.

'Sorry.'

'For what?' Voit enquired.

But Tristram could not say.

It somehow came out of that altercation. Perhaps it was something Voit said that evening, although it felt as if it had been building in him for some time, a need for redress, for compensation of a sort. Not revenge, he would never use that word.

'But a balancing?' Voit suggested as they strolled across Szabadság square. 'Then that is our goal and our destination.'

He pointed.

The rear of the Hotel Ikrek rose above the park, self-absorbed and crowned by a penthouse suite that resembled the pagoda of some especially aloof and grandiose potentate. Lights shone behind curtains and broad panes of translucent glass. No sign of life nor hint of the opulence sure to be found inside.

'Guarded, needless to say,' Voit murmured, nodding to a society lady walking her tiny dog.

'But not unassailable?' They began to stroll once more, up and down.

'What is?'

And so it was decided. They would break into Nox's suite.

The hotel receptionist called them back before they got halfway to the lift.

'Frau Lang left no instructions.'

Voit looked confused. 'The Langs? Suit 109, the top floor?'

'Yes but I was not aware it was Frau Lang's birthd—'

Voit made an anxious hushing gesture. 'I understand she is most sensitive on the mater. *Tempus fugit*, even for one so young at heart.' Voit nodded at Tristram to start walking. 'We must not delay any longer. Our thanks, good sir—'

'But lilies?'

'They are Herr Lang's instructions and Frau Lang's favourites.' Voit inspected the lobby for eavesdroppers. 'I am given to understand she suffers from a morbid affliction— fear of mortality, ageing. I know nothing of the details, good sir. We merely deliver flowers and arrange them in such a way as to give the poor woman some pleasure on this otherwise traumatic day.'

The receptionist's gaze settled on Tristram. 'You don't look like florists.'

Tristram tried to hide behind the armfuls of lilies he carried, aware of the state of his suit, the cardboard shoes, the razor rash blossoming across his freshly shaven face.

Voit drew himself up to his full height. 'We,' he enunciated, 'are expected. I doubt Herr Lang wishes to be kept waiting, on this evening of all evenings, his wife in so delicate a state and—'

The receptionist wavered.

'Be sure to report to me before you leave. Now be quick about it.' He waved a finger in the direction of the lift. 'Herr

Lang is waiting.'

The flowers filled the lift car with the stink of mildew. The operator acted as if nothing strange was happening.

Decision made, they had both thought it would be easy to find out the habits of Nox and his entourage. But the hotel staff proved silent on the topic with no bribe nor persuasion enough to get anyone they approached to offer anything, even the filmiest scrap of gossip.

'Perhaps when they leave the hotel?'

They sat beside the fire in the communal living room, evening blinking as it pinned up its hair and readied for the night to come.

'An ambush?' Voit shuddered. 'I do not have your soldier's taste for head-on confrontation, my dearest Tristram. It strikes me as hazardous. Now to sneak in to the hotel, sneak out...'

Tristram glanced up. Sára was watching them as she sat at the table.

'Yes, I suppose.' Tristram grimaced, on the verge of throwing over the whole idea.

But, later that evening, Sára came into the bar and told them she had struck up a friendship with a garrulous porter at the Hotel Ikrek, a man very discontented with his wife and only too happy to have someone to flatter and praise him.

'What do you want to know?' she asked.

Voit clapped. Tristram had said nothing. But, next evening, he stood on the threshold of her room, as she dabbed on make-up scavenged from a dozen different places, and asked:

'Are you sure?'

It was the porter's night off; they were to meet within the hour.

'You want to know, don't you?' She pouted into the mirror. He saw himself in the corner of the glass; Sára did not meet his reflection.

'Yes. But...'

'Hm?'

'Yes.' He turned sharply away, throat tight. 'Thank you.'

Three nights after that, the porter accidentally found his girlfriend in a passionate embrace with the commis chef and broke up with her then and there.

Sára declined Voit's offer of gin and concentrated on drawing plans: penthouse floor plan, stairs, fire exits.

One of the card players gave a yell of triumph. The barman dropped a glass.

'Capital.' Voit was delighted.

'Sára?'

She was halfway to the corner before Tristram got to the door.

She stopped walking but did not turn. 'Your Lordship?'

'I wanted...' An impulse tugged his hand from his pocket, leaving the coins there, certain, no matter how he tried, any offer of payment would be misunderstood. 'To thank you. Again. For... this.'

'It's what your Lordship wants most, isn't it?'

She took his silence as a yes.

'Well, there you are then.'

She continued walking and he let her go. The following evening, after rifling Kerepesi Cemetery of flowers, he and Voit were bluffing their way into the hotel lift, to be carried to the penthouse.

The lift doors parted.

They set off in the direction the operator showed them, the Lang's suit waiting at the far end of a long corridor lined with thickets of potted palms and ferns and so thickly carpeted their footsteps made no sound.

Behind them, the lift doors swung shut and the winding gear began to hum.

Within moments, the lilies were stuffed into several of

the plant pots and they were heading back, past the main lifts, down a long, narrow branch that let into a side corridor leading back, behind the lift shaft. To another, smaller, private lift. And a door, stairwell beyond. Tristram tried the door.

Not locked. Just as the porter had told Sára.

'I think it would be better—'

Voit raised a hand. 'We have discussed at length, my friend. They do no know me. Should anything go awry, I may say something to divert suspicion. But you, you who they have seen and know of, you must wait here.'

'But—'

'No, no, as we have discussed,' Voit said and let himself into the stairwell.

Tristram crossed his arms, squeezing against his hands. Anything to stop them shaking.

As much as the porter had been happy to gossip about the guests on the tenth floor, he most liked to talk about the couple and their entourage staying in the penthouse above. The private lift needed a key. So should the stairs but the key had been lost ages ago and, anyway, there were guards in the lobby where the lift and the stairs came out. Guards with tommy guns, watched over by Nox's chief, a thug called Floyd who had been a bootlegger and a hired gunman and had worked for Al Capone. So it didn't matter that you could get up the stairs. Except, each evening, Nox took Alba out, dinner or a casino or a nightclub, the guards going with them, suit vacant for hours on end. The porter told Sára he had gone up the back stairs to the penthouse loads of times. He had stolen Nox's cigars and drunk Nox's brandy…

The stairwell door remained closed, did not open to let Voit through to announce that the penthouse was empty.

Restlessness forced Tristram to pace back and forth; a few paces before returning to the door before turning away to walk another few paces. He counted the seconds, calculating times reasonable and less so. He almost snatched open the stairwell door, wanting to dash up to the penthouse, regardless of plans or gangsters, anything to put an end to this.

Yet he held to the space of those few paces, ears twitching at each slight noise, unwilling to give up, for Voit's sake, unwilling to rush upstairs. Tristram could not say why.

A smell, faint and acrid, drifted along the corridor, stronger on the second breath, smell of burning more noticeable the closer he got to the lift shaft.

The lift began to whir.

Tristram leapt back a step. Feet not quite coming back to the carpet: hanging, suspended: between darting into the stairwell and retreating to the main corridor; by the thought that Voit might have discovered the key.

The lift doors opened. Wiry, pinstripe jacket hanging open, looking like it might have been dragged on in a hurry. A shock of red hair.

Dumbstruck, gazes meeting. Neither sure how to react.

At last, seconds or a year later, a look of recognition widened the red-haired man's eyes as, an instant later, Tristram realised this was one of the guards who had gone to drag Voit away from the bandstand at the nightclub.

If he acted, in this very split second, he could take the man by surprise—

Jacket snatched aside, right hand plunging, hauling out a heavy automatic pistol.

Tristram's feet touched carpet. He darted for the stairwell after all, deafening bark and muzzle flash left behind, bullet burying itself deep into the wall—

Bang.

Wrenching open the door, he plunged across the landing, a second bullet splintering the doorframe as a third corkscrewed through the diminishing space between his head and the closing door, breath of passage silent because there was no time to register anything, beyond the near miss and the icicle stab that there were two gunmen in the lift, the red-head not alone. Two men. Neither Voit—

The stairwell roiled. Air choking the breath from him as it clutched at his face and pawed at his eyes. Tristram hit the guard rail. Almost lost his balance, almost pitched over to fall through the smoke. Fell the other way instead. Flight slamming each last scrap of breath from him. Bump, bump, bump—

'He went up!'

The door banged, bump, bump.

'Down. Went over the handrail. Shit—'

Flame stretched a hand downwards from the direction of the penthouse, growling and barking, spewing another gout of smoke, angry, and hungry.

Tristram blinked, pain of impact and thickening smoke spilling tears down his face. His shoulder complained, loud and bitter, hip and thigh likewise insisting he should crawl away as a fast as possible. Ignoring them both, he tried to make sense of the shapes on the landing above. Light and smoke. Flames dancing. Shouts from above. Yelling, but mute. The sound of the flames.

'Forget him. We should—'

Light from the door opening, smoke batting it aside, wanting all this for itself.

'But— Crap, there—'

Shape and flash and bullet ricochet all in the space of one choked breath. Rolling, cringing away from plaster scattering, next bullet going wide. Footfalls on the stairs.

Bump, bump.

Tristram turning fall into stumble, managing to turn that into a career, step to step, balance not quite lost in the thickening smoke.

The door was reluctant to give way but it opened and he tumbled into the corridor beyond. Potted plants. Open doors. Voices. Figures in evening wear or their night things. Bellboys pointing towards the main stairs. A sense of urgency, not panic, not yet. Looking, face to face, searching for Voit, going with the tide a few steps before ducking out to look along the lines of guests filing out, looking for Voit. And knowing he had to go back, could not leave.

He turned, hurrying back towards the stair doors.

'Sir? Sir! You must evacuate—'

Tristram turned at the voice. A bellboy pointing down the length of the hallway.

'This way.'

'Yes. I've just forgotten something. Won't be a moment.'

'This—'

'A moment—' Tristram pressed forward, a shape seen from the corner of his eye, too late to avoid collision, shape sent backwards, into one of the palms, pot stand overturning and bringing the shape to the floor with it.

'Sorry, I—'

Nox's red-haired guard, flat on his back. Swearing. Pot overturned, pot stand across his legs. Gun just a little way from his groping hand.

Tristram made a grab as the guard kicked the stand off his legs.

Almost knocking the gun away. Almost.

Gun cold and heavy, hard to keep steady so he needed both hands to take a bead on the red haired guard.

Just the two of them. Corridor clear. No sign of his comrades.

The other man's eyes widened, seconds dragging out, time enough for him to look into the barrel, to lick his lips. Point blank range, as good as. Impossible to miss. Tristram relaxed and the muzzle fixed itself on the centre of the man's chest.

No doubt how this would go if the sides were reversed.

Tristram cocked the pistol.

The red-haired man closed his eyes.

The gun bucked. Plaster showering them both.

Tristram lowered the pistol until it was aimed at the guard again.

'Don't follow me,' he whispered. 'Next time, I won't aim at the ceiling.'

No time for a reply. He turned and ran.

He haunted the lobby for as long as possible, hiding the pistol deep inside an ornamental flower pot before filing out to mill with the crowds watching the top floors of the Hotel Ikrek burn. Despite the heat, he shivered. Despite knowing, no matter how indirectly, he was responsible for this fire, he felt nothing. Only that he had to find Voit.

Voit was not among the hotel guests being ushered away from the building. No sign of him, either, amongst the crowd. Perhaps Voit had already escaped. Tristram could not turn away from the fire, staring up at the flames that had replaced the penthouse and which crept, floor by floor, downwards. He could not leave. He had to know. And so he began to worm through the crowd, anxious to get to the front. Thoughts vague so he had no idea how he would get into the building again, or how he would be able to search the burning floors.

A policeman turned to him as he tried to cross the road.

'Oi!'

Tristram froze, unable to move forward or back. For a moment or so, he was certain the policeman had guessed his involvement in the fire but the officer simply told him to get back with everyone else, threatening to charge him with a breach of the peace when Tristram still could not make his legs work.

'Ruddy gawpers.' The policeman waved his hand again. 'Go on, buzz off, haven't you seen enough?' He waited, hands on hips, until Tristram stumbled through the first few rows of spectators.

Skirting the rear of the crowd, Tristram circled until he could cross the road again, glancing up the length of Hold utca, towards the corner with Báthory.

'Please, would you help me?'

He did not react to the voice at first, intent on returning to the hotel.

'Please…'

Soot stained her pale skin, her hair turned grey with ash.

'Please, I can pay…'

Her dress was smirched, as stained as the crumpled bank

66

notes tumbling from her outstretched hands. She shivered, the night frigid with the promise of snow.

He pushed the notes away, hurriedly draping his jacket across her shoulders. 'I know somewhere,' he whispered, telling himself the stammer was the cold and nothing but the cold. 'It's a little far but it's not a difficult walk.'

'I can't go far.'

And that was when Tristram saw the links wound around Alba's ankle.

II
ALBEDO

THE DAWN TURNED to him as he climbed the steps, its soft white robes making no sound as it raised a finger to its lips to ask for quiet. Fresh snow had fallen overnight. No sign of yesterday's footprints, no sign of yesterday. He crossed the pavement, paused in the middle of the empty road, the snow in front of him featureless, as if this were the first time he had walked here. The church craned over the crumbling wall enclosing the graveyard to see him through the half-shadows, sun still not yet clear of the lip of the world, although the snow clouds glowed faintly, a soft, internal light that set the great onion dome capping the bell tower glistening.

Nothing moved. Not here. Not in the city of Pest. Not in the whole world.

Tristram bent his head, eyes closed. Listening, his breath held until, faintly, at the very furthest tip of hearing, he caught the sound of snow crystals, one settling against another. Whispering.

His boots crunched as he turned a circle, fresh prints to mark the day's first survey of the terrain, down the length of Szerb utca towards the crossroads, cold air making his eyes smart, biting against the stubble on his scalp, noticeable because he was yet to get used to such close-cropped hair, just as he was getting used to the thickening beard and moustaches, Tristram no longer easy to recognise on casual glance. Not quite the man he had been a few weeks ago.

Nothing moved other than a street dog that ambled out of a doorway to stand and look at him looking.

Tristram nodded. The dog sat and made no other move. Somewhere, wings beat against the slate grey air. And, in the very distance, a clink of tack suggested a horse and cart, sound lost a moment later by the deep drone of an engine, a lorry moaning to itself at having to be up and about so early, in all this snow, and the sun not yet up...

And so, shrugging deeper into his greatcoat, collar drawn up about his ears, Tristram began to walk. Like yesterday morning, and the day before and the day before. Walking the bounds of his protectorate. A sentry on patrol.

They had run, from the fire and the alarm bells, from the growl of an engine that might have been encased in a chassis of black and white. Alba favoured her right leg, the one with the chain, foot dragging and causing her pain. Tristram gripped her arm, almost carrying her as they tottered into the park behind the blazing Ikrek, path set to take them towards The Toad Pond, the Danube waiting a little beyond that. 'Buda?' he gasped. He did not know Buda, had never been there, but the notion of being out of this city seemed the only solution. 'Could you make it across the river?' Alba winced, almost fell against him, but she nodded, 'I think so,' and it seemed she grew heavier against his arm, her right foot dragging and the tiny links of gold and of silver glinting under the streetlights.

But, when they stumbled to the end of Széchenyi utca, found the Danube crawling through the darkness, the spires and domes of Buda staring back at them from the hills on the opposite bank, it was Tristram who faltered, stomach hollowed and turned icy, the next breath harder to find than the last.

'Too far.' Széchenyi Bridge five-hundred metres further upstream, its arches just visible beyond the trees lining the banks.

'I can—'

'No.' Tristram pulled Alba in the opposite direction. Telling her he could hear bells, an engine.

The Danube said nothing.

They stumbled past the Parliament building, ornate and filled with dreams the people of Hungary had long ago abandoned, into the streets to the north, orderly and regular and increasingly anonymous. A good place to hide, Tristram thought, turning his back on the Danube and the city that rested on its far bank, bells and alarms distant, flames hardly burnishing the clouds. Even the sounds of engines waned.

Tristram took a little of Alba's money ('I stole it,' she whispered, 'from *him*, he does not know') and got them a room in a scruffy hotel that skulked between a pawn broker's and a tailor's, Tristram keeping Alba hidden although the night manager never looked up from his newspaper, taking and pocketing the money with one hand as he licked a finger, turned a page with the other. He yawned, settled back to reading.

'He will find us.' Alba refused to go into the room at first, wanting to keep running.

'You can't run any further. And how can he find us?' Tristram managed to settle her beside the wheezing radiator and wrapped the bed's only blanket around her shoulders. The feeble glow from the single bulb dangling from the ceiling pointed out a blue tinge in her skin, charcoal smudges under her eyes that were not soot from the fire. Tears ran through the dirt on her face. She laughed, shook her head. Cried more, hugging herself as she rocked on the creaking chair.

Tristram fretted. Going to check the door was locked. Going to check the catch on the only window was secure (it was broken, but the window was painted shut in any case). He sat on the edge of the bed. Wanting to suggest she sleep, that they both rest. Impressions from the evening argued against rest; each one smelled of smoke and was anxious with fear, each one speaking with the voice of the flames chewing away at the penthouse. At Voit—

'Your husband escaped the fire?'

'Who?' Her hair fell across her face.

'Your husband. Nox.'

'He is not my husband.' Alba stopped rocking. 'He is not. He is not,' she shouted, fists white as they beat the air.

He hushed her. Pleaded that they must be quite, must not draw attention to themselves. Ordered her to shut up and be calm. Alba grew more agitated and Tristram hurriedly apologised, gabbling words, anything to placate her.

'I'm sorry. I was told, I heard that— I don't understand—'

'Nox. Attar Nox.' Alba enunciated with deliberate emphasis. 'Is. My. *Brother*.'

Pest woke around him, pavements filling, vans and cars huffing over having to trudge through so much new snow, lights flickering on in shopfronts and behind apartment windows. He looked for a flash of black and white, or for a face that might be too intent and watchful. Somewhere in the clouds, beyond rime-dressed roofs, an aeroplane droned.

Like yesterday, Tristram thought, pausing at the next corner, a street hawker stoic when Tristram repeated that he needed no gloves. A motor car. A woman slipping on impacted snow turned to ice, fur coat pulled close about her. Part of him relaxed, moment by moment, as nothing threatening appeared. Part of him grew more clenched, but for the self same reason, minute by minute coming to admit that, here at least, there was nothing to worry about. *Like yesterday.*

He started the return leg. Once, he had carried on from this spot, walking northwards until the remains of the Hotel Ikrek pulled themselves upright, shaking off a dusting of snow, snow coating the scaffolding helping it stand, icicles bristling from blacked crossbeams, the smell of cinder lost under the scent of frost. The carcass of the building sucked in the light from the drab sky, becoming featureless, easy to think he was staring into a deep hole down which Voit had fallen and vanished.

Tristram had waited, conscious of time's passing and waiting a little longer, a little while longer. But Voit neither climbed out of that abyss of scorched wood and stone, nor stepped from behind a tree or out a nearby doorway, any more than he had stepped out of the house at the end of Holló átjáó when he and Alba had found their way there, first floor windows boarded over, building untenanted, abandoned.

Like yesterday—and the day before and the day before and the day before—he followed a route that paralleled the Danube for a short way, but lined up the intervening buildings to block all view of the river and the city squatting on its far bank. Instead, Tristram saw passing motorcars, buildings with high rooftops reassuringly empty of observers, corner idlers swathed in scarves of their own breath, or the smoke of cigarettes cupped in their hands. None of it suspicious, all of it familiar from the day before and the day before and the day before...

And still he patrolled. And still he kept watch.

The old beggar was passing the gate to the graveyard as Tristram rounded the corner into Szerb utca. White cane groping a path through the snow to the low niche in the wall, beggar sitting, head craned towards the first flakes ushering along a new flurry. The breeze tugged at white hair spilling from beneath a battered felt hat, the old beggar pretending not to hear Tristram approaching. But nostrils twitched as the breeze carried the scent of bread, fresh from the bakery two streets over, to the niche, and the beggar sat a little straighter.

Tristram tore a hunk off the loaf.

'Here you are, father.' He pressed the bread into one of the beggar's hands, finding a few coppers in his pocket to tuck into the other.

'Thank you.'

'Keep watch.'

The beggar nodded.

Alba had woke, screaming.

'He is here... He is here...'

Tristram had leapt from where he had been sleeping on the floor, running into the wall before finding the door handle, sure Nox must already in the room.

The scruffy hotel room's door was locked.

She clutched her leg, bed frame complaining as she writhed to kick away the blankets knotted around her. 'Do not let him take me,' Alba begged. 'I will not be taken, do not let him...'

He wanted to tell her it was a dream. When he unpicked the blankets, the weak light pointed to her ankle, skin swollen and livid, thin chain of silver and gold drawn tight and biting deeper and deeper into her flesh. He forgot what he had been

75

about to say.

Alba could barely walk, leg dragging. He helped her down the stairs and she felt heavier, no longer the wraith she had been but a being of lead and stone. The stairs groaned each time Alba managed to drag her right foot down another step.

The chain bit deeper.

They found a back way out of the hotel, into an alley, Alba too exhausted to walk and Tristram carrying her, almost collapsing under the weight as the chain grew tighter.

She gripped his sleeve, clutching the flesh beneath.

'He is here, please, I cannot be with him again, I cannot…'

At the end of the alley a rickety door opened on to the main boulevard.

'Wait.' Easing her into the shadow cast by a shop's deep doorway.

'No—'

He dashed back to the junction with the road the hotel faced on to, slowing to peer around the corner.

The black and white limousine was parked towards the far end, engine spewing clouds of smoke. Shapes approached along both sides of the street. Checking each building. Red hair flashed under one of the streetlamps, figure hardly glancing at the pawn broker's but stopping to read the scruffy hotel's nameplate, waving, one of the limousine's back doors opening, a form tall and dark and cruel unfolding itself…

They ran. Alba stumbling, desperation and Tristram between them carrying her, the weight of the thin ankle chain trying to fix them to one place for Nox to find. That weight ebbed, little on little, leaving an exhaustion almost as heavy. Tristram looked over his shoulder, no longer sure where they were. A new day was forming, reeking of iron and grinding every line and curve of the city to a razor edge.

'He is no longer so close,' Alba gasped, the chain the only thing anchoring her to the pavement, skin pale, a cloud of mist that might evaporate any moment.

They found another hotel, at the bottom of a narrow alley that offered escape in at least two directions. He wanted to ask about the chain, needed to stay awake and watch, wrapping his jacket about her, telling her she must rest, that it was safe.

Alba nodded. 'For now.'

Rain that yearned to be sleet peppered the window. Tristram blinked, unable to stop shivering, dreams and memories too firmly tangled to unpick, so there was no telling if he had slept a minute or several hours.

Alba's foot stuck out from beneath the thin blanket, pale skin livid against the grey of the bed sheet where the chain had bitten deep. The links hung loosely. Except, in the next moment, they slithered with the motion of a snake hunting prey, flexing and tightening, the renewed pressure waking Alba. Neither spoke, saving their breath to run.

A glimpse of black and white limousine. Shouts. City teetering, about to fall apart. Nowhere safe. A glimpse of red hair. Of overcoat and brown fedora, a pistol. All to the roar of an engine. No breath to spare, only run. Alba stumbling. Alba falling. Sweating, hands shaking. Swearing. At gun metal clouds and a pavement unyielding. At the whirl of motorcars and trams, at not being able to tell black from white. Hands sweating, shaking. Expecting whistles, bodies thrown back into the trench, shrapnel and bullets and the flames of a penthouse burning with revenge, cold to the touch, cold as a face on the other side of a room, a memory it was too late to push away.

'Leave me. I am sorry I placed you in this—'

'Hush.' His hands were steady, firm but, as much as haste and need allowed, gentle as he picked Alba up, arm around her waist, hefting the weight of the chain and adjusting his grip. 'You asked for my help.'

'But, please…' Tears glistened, freshened themselves. Eyes deep within fields of grey. 'I cannot ask— You do not—'

'I want to help.'

They hid, behind dustbins and piles of wooden crates that smelled of the dark earth far beneath the cobbles and tarmacadam, the clatter of pans coming from the restaurant's open door to look at them, going back inside to bring out one of the washers-up. He shrugged, disappeared to return, handing a loaf to Tristram, a packet of cured sausage following. The Head Chef was a turd, the washer-up warned them, but he was busy yelling at the manager of the restaurant, so they could stay another half hour, if they wanted. He pressed a bowl of tea into Alba's hands, waved, and retreated along the alley to smoke.

The pain from the ankle chain grew fractionally easier; Nox was searching somewhere less close-by.

Two hours later, they hobbled down Raven Passage.

'There are people who will help,' Tristram repeated.

But the house acted as if it had never met Tristram before. Boards closed the mouth of the front door, grime and stillness clogged the gutters and welded shut the windows, those that were not broken. Nevertheless, he hammered on the door, clambered up on to the wall to see into the yard at the rear, tried to climb across to one of the first floor windows. The whole place was abandoned and might have stood this way for a week or a year.

The house on Raven Passage turned them away.

'Perhaps if we cross the river?'

'It's too far.' He shook his head.

'Perhaps…' Alba kneaded at her leg, muscles twitching from carrying the weight of the chain. The links were not biting but the weight was growing worse: they were drawing close to the limits of her free movement. Keep going and the weight would increase, and increase.

Tristram turned away. They sat on the curb of a side street lined with tall houses, apartments and flats, neither grand nor dowdy. There seemed little point in hiding.

There seemed little point.

Speed. And distance. These were the things they needed and had none of.

Tristram straightened, peering at the nearest street sign. 'Where are we?'

Alba made no reply, not even a shrug.

It was a ridiculous thought. The chain would never allow it, any more than Nox would. 'We must try,' Tristram coaxed. Alba could hardly stand without falling. 'It can't be more than a handful of streets from here.' Tristram put his arm around her waist, the bones and sinews beneath his borrowed jacket and her soot-stained dress more ragged and spare than they had been hours earlier. Last night, an æon gone by and taking this day with it.

Dusk mobbed the sky above József Boulevard, air growing thick as it grew colder, motor exhaust mixing with the sharp tang of impending snow. The boulevard thronged, streetlamps beginning to kindle amidst noise and bustle, foot and wheel. No sign of black and white, not low growl or the click of a gun being cocked. Alba hung back before they could step off the pavement.

'This will not work.'

'But it might be a barrier.'

'The weight—'

'Can't build forever.' A memory of whistles, the ladder muddy under his hands, and a face turning away without comment, which was comment enough. 'Please, Alba, while your brother is searching somewhere else. Unless he's given up?' No way to keep that slim hope from returning.

Alba shook her head.

They stepped into the throng. Keleti railway station, single, huge fan window of steel and glass a Cyclops's eye, half-closed and unblinking above the tangles of omnibuses and motorcars and pedestrians. Tristram willed the station closer with each faltering step they managed, reassuring himself the first express train out of the city was the answer. Speed and distance would beat Nox, he reminded himself.

'Tristram—'

The steps up to the main entrance were dead ahead. The station's busiest time, hundreds flowed back and forth.

'Tristram—'

Alba was no weight at all. Amidst all these people, Nox could never find them.

'Almost there.' He carried her up the steps, under the Cyclops eye, the central station enclosing them, crowds and bedlam and the hiss of steam and the slow pulse of trains pulling in, trains gaining speed to dart away along the tracks ranging from the rear of the station. Endless.

'I cannot—' She clawed at his neck, pulling him down as she collapsed. 'The pain—'

'She ain't goin' nowhere, mac.' The voice came out of the churning crowd, grew solid: a man in long overcoat and brown fedora, pistol appearing in his hand. 'An' neither are you. Give it up, buddy.'

'Floyd.' The name hardly even a breath.

'Missus.' Floyd touched the brim of his hat, other hand holding the pistol close to his body, hard to notice, unlikely to miss at this range. Tristram glanced around. Recognising a face from the nightclub beating, another nearby. The red-haired gangster from the hotel stepped from behind a chattering family lugging suitcases bound by lengths of rope.

'Do like Floyd says,' the red-haired man advised, hands in the pockets of his coat, revolver, no doubt, trained through the folds of cloth. He titled his head towards the station entrance. Through the to and fro, a figure appeared, unhurried.

Attar Nox.

Alba sobbed. 'Tristram—'

He tensed, no plan in mind other than to act.

A pistol cocked. 'Don't try it.' Floyd stepped closer. 'This crowd ain't gonna stop me plugging you. Get me?'

The crowd flowed around Nox, around the bodyguards flanking him, stream water around rocks. A smile settling into Nox's features, cruel and triumphant. He drew breath.

A figure doddered out of the crowd, into Nox's path, a tray of wears clipping one of the guards, showering laces and matches and sprigs of lucky lavender in all directions.

'Get lost, lady—'

'You'll pay for them!' The street hawker lashed out at the bodyguard, her hand catching Nox across the face before he had time to duck. A second bodyguard rushed in. Staggering, station lights skittering across the lenses of her smoked glasses, the hawker swung around, her old felt hat knocked off, white hair coming loose. Her tray came up and it could only be dumb luck, she was blind after all, but the edge caught the lunging guard hard across the face, blood spattering from his nose, tray corner following through, into Nox's chest, the blind woman falling back a step and her foot raking against the shin of the first guard as he rummaged beneath his coat, revolver snagged on the lining.

Floyd had time to swear, no more, before a whistle shrilled across the concourse, a second policeman bursting out of one of little eateries and coffee bars lining one side of the tracks.

The red-haired man turned towards the yelling street hawker, the other hoodlums frozen by surprise.

Tristram had no memory of starting to walk. No idea how he had lifted Alba, half-carried her towards a side entrance, not looking back no matter how loud the yelling, how shrill and many the police whistles. Slowly becoming conscious, the further they walked, that Alba was able to carry more and more of her own weight, that weight growing less.

They paused, Alba leaning a hand against a lamp post as she turned her foot, line bitten by the chain angry and swollen, the chain itself snug but no longer burying itself in her flesh.

'He is gone,' she whispered.

The tower and the onion dome turned towards them as they wandered along Szerb utca. An iron gate in the high wall let them look into the enclosure around the church, steps leading down to a path, trees and bushes, the last of the night stealing between the gravestones, pausing to glance towards Alba, a finger to its lips. Sparrows in the yew trees stirred, whispering to each other but not breaking the hush.

It began to snow.

Alba pushed open the iron gate, following the path until it lead her to a bench set against the high enclosure wall.

Tristram watched the last of the night drain away into a morning of pewter and pearl. The sparrows found their voice. Alba tilted back her head, eyes closed as snow flakes gently kissed her forehead and cheeks. After a little longer, he crossed the street to look at the To Let sign he had noticed earlier, a basement room opposite the church, landlord's address three streets away, landlord himself in a tavern, drinking his breakfast beer, eyeing each coin of the three weeks' rent Tristram counted out. 'Card game,' Tristram mumbled, 'got lucky.' The landlord shrugged, shrugged again when Tristram answer yes, he did live alone. 'Don't care 'oo you live wiv,' the landlord grunted, handing Tristram the key.

They bought second-hand clothes for themselves—greatcoat, stout boots, thick workman's trousers for him; two dresses, plain and heavy, thick woollen stockings, a headscarf and a cardigan for her—blankets and pots and pans for the basement room: grate and stove and a sink with a hand pump, a narrow bed opposite a half-moon window through which the church spire could look through if it ducked its domed head a little. Tristram insisted on sleeping beneath the window. 'Nox has gone,' Alba whispered, chain no longer painful. 'Yes,' he agreed, blowing out the candle and staying awake until he was sure she was sleeping. Come morning, before sunrise, he had pulled on the greatcoat and gone out to find the city draped in white, each footstep crunching has made his first patrol of their tiny estate.

The fire recited its vespers.

'Tell me about yourself.'

Plates lay between them on the threadbare rug, supper almost done.

'Oh… Such as?' He took the poker and churned the logs and clinker in the grate. The fire paused until he finished before returning to its evening prayers. Sparks drifted in constellations unnamed.

'Anything.' Alba settled a blanket around her shoulders, basement room chilly in spite of the fire, drawing her knees up beneath her skirt. She dabbed a crumb from her plate. 'Where you were born, why you came to this city, anything at all. I know nothing about you, Tristram.'

'Well…' Tristram managed to balance his plate on his crossed legs, cleaning the last streaks of gravy with a scrap of bread. 'Well…' He chewed, unable to think of anything that seemed grand enough or in any way significant. Head bent over the last of dinner, his gaze strayed to Alba, the fire reaching out to weave rose gold through her hair, lay shadows in such a way that made her eyes gleam.

'Well,' he began again, fire's glow making him, of a sudden, very warm indeed. Concentrating on collecting the last smears of gravy the bread, Tristram talked a little about his childhood in Wales—'I was adopted, I never knew my actual mother and father'—mentioned volunteering to fight in the War, room growing hotter by the moment. He shuffled back a little from the fire, put his plate on to the rug beside Alba's plate, only to find he had nothing to do with his hands. Tristram took back the plate and the spoon. 'After that, I worked for a bank,' his finished lamely.

'And that is what bought you to Budapest?' As she spoke, Alba rose to heft the iron tea pot from its spot by the fire and hold it out in invitation.

'Yes.' Tristram found his cup. Fumes rose from the hot tea. He shivered and moved closer to the fire again. 'And now I'm stranded. The Crash…' He explained, the story of his faith in his employers slowly turning to lead and mire sounding ridiculous to him. 'I was a fool, a bloody naïve fool.' His throat closed, tea hard to swallow. Tristram put the cup aside.

'But you had no reason to distrust them.'

'I went on trusting them for too long.' Trying to keep the thickness out of his voice and failing. 'I'm sorry. I'm sure you don't want to hear me moaning. You've got problems of your own, much bigger ones.'

But Alba would not let him leave it, would not allow that her problems were greater. Tristram found himself admitting how greatly he was stranded.

'You have no one'

Tristram took the tea pot, offering to make fresh.

'No one at all?'

'Vivien.'

The admission caught him by surprise. He had thought to say nothing, let the conversation die.

'Your…' Alba added a piece of wood to the fire. 'Your wife?'

'Fiancée.' The silence seemed brittle against his skin. 'A very beautiful woman,' Tristram added and thought it the wrong thing to say the moment he spoke.

'You must miss her very much. I am sorry.' Alba threw another piece of wood on the fire. 'She cannot help you?'

'No.' After a moment, Tristram put the kettle aside, brisk and businesslike as he spoke. 'It's getting late.' He hauled on the greatcoat. 'I should patrol one last time.'

'It is so cold tonight. I am sure there is no need.'

'It's for the best,' he repeated, softly closing the door behind him before Alba had chance to speak.

Days came to the basement door and left without offering sign of Nox or mention of Voit. The red wheal faded from Alba's leg, chain remaining no more than links of gold and silver against her skin. She did not rouse when he left each dawn; if she dreamt, she dreamt peacefully and her cries no longer woke him in the night as he lay beneath the half-moon window. In the late morning, or the early afternoon, whenever the snow grew slack and faded into the lustreless sky, Alba crossed to the church behind its wall, tower and onion dome grizzled, iron gate squeaking a *hullo* as she followed her footprints between the trees and the graves that peeked out of low drifts, clearing snow from the bench between two yews, a robin complaining at the intrusion, falling silent as stillness returned to the churchyard, Alba sitting peacefully, content to watch the breeze through the branches, the city's obsessive maundering growing distant.

Tristram sat in the niche in the outside wall. Sometimes, the blind beggar was already there and they sat, silent, the caw of a crow , or a street dog nosing around the stairs to the basement flat, pulling Tristram out of his reveries.

Days went by.

Tristram lolled in his makeshift bed, resentful of another dawn peering through the chink in the thin curtains, another day coming to their door. Sour at seeing Alba sleeping deeply, banked fire weaving warmth around her bed, curtain making sure the new day could not quite touch her, left her in peace. He shook his head. Cursed himself for the fool he was. And shooed the new day aside so he could pull the door closed behind him. Gently, silently.

The city rubbed sleep from its eyes and watched him: past the church to the crossroads with Verse Pálné utca, then left or right or straight on, on a whim because he knew he should vary his route. Snow settled on his shoulders, anointed the stubble on his scalp, beard fuller and better able to keep the cold at bay. Tristram caught sight of himself in a window and, for a heartbeat or so, convinced himself he did not recognise the man in the reflection.

A dog barked.

A magpie clacked.

Cars and vans grumbled through the snow, drifts heaving themselves up along each gutter, white on white, hardly any shadows to be seen, clouds capping the roofs of Pest glowing faintly with snow yet to come. Tristram paused, smells from a café mingling with motor exhaust, neither quite managing to banish the sharp tang of snow and chill. Part of him relaxed, moment by moment. Part of him clenched until the resentment became a sour taste in the mouth.

An engine droned overhead. He scanned the sky between the buildings but, after another minute, gave up looking, the aeroplane obviously flying above the clouds.

Second thoughts pushed aside, Tristram slithered across icy pavements, crossing the city until he reached Hold utca and the remains of the Hotel Ikrek, its charred face dressed in white now, the shell fading into the snow as it was beginning to fade in memory. Voit was lost; Tristram could never know any more about the night he met Alba than he already knew or than she had told him: waking from a doze, hearing shouts, the scent and sight of smoke, being bundled from her room, hallways filled with fumes and the sound of flames, the confusion mounting along with the certainty that she had to act even if the thought of action made her sick...

Tristram turned his back on the Ikrek. He would not come here again.

The second-hand bookshop made no attempt to stop him as he walked by. Still, Tristram paused, indecision gone in a rush, only to come back as he looked at the piles of books, spines merging and their titles refusing to settle as his gaze skimmed from shelf to shelf. He chose almost at random, hoping it truly was a prod of intuition that caused him to pick up the two novels, sifting through the coins in his pocket, conscious he was using Alba's money to buy her presents.

She waved his excuses and apologies away, smiling as she looked through each book, turning the pages of one before setting it aside to sample the other.

'Read to me?' She held out the novel. 'Please, Tristram?'

More excuses, filling his head and crowding for chance to come out. Wanting to say he was too busy making them breakfast. Knowing such a thing would be ridiculous and rude and still wavering, until, unable to meet her gaze, or look directly at the smile on her face, he took the book.

Tristram cleared his throat.

'Chapter One...'

Early evening.

'Tell me about yourself.'

Alba looked up as Tristram held out a bowl of stew. The fire paused over its vespers.

'Oh… Such as?' she asked, taking the goulash and setting it beside the grate until he had got a bowl for himself and settled in his spot on the rug.

'Anything.' Tristram blew across the bowl, steam scented with paprika and caraway, winter greens mixed among potatoes, peppers and carrots. Alba did not eat meat. Tristram thought he was beginning to adapt.

'Well…' She tested a spoonful, blowing hard and trying again until she could eat without scalding herself. 'I suppose you're curious about Attar.'

He watched her eat, searching for any sign of tension, reluctance and, seeing none, allowed, 'I am curious,' before hurrying to add, 'Although it's none of my business, of course, I don't wish—'

'My adopted brother.' Alba tore a little bread and scooped up gravy. She looked at the fire and the fire ducked its gaze, beginning its evening prayers over again.

Goulash turning acid in his stomach, Tristram drew breath, ready to change the subject. But Alba continued.

I was very young when my mother and father adopted me. I think I have dim memories of my parents, my real parents. I'm not sure. My home—my adopted home—was a castle, deep in the forest. I thought it was enchanted, a fairy tale castle, when I first saw it. It was the only world I knew for a long time, Tristram. I thought it was normal, the shadows of the trees and the high walls, the chill and dank of the corridors, the raised voices and the silences.

(Alba ate a little of the goulash and Tristram wanted to change the subject again. Before he could speak—)

I had been an only child. Now I had brothers. There was Nox, who is a few years older than I, and there was his older brother, who seemed very grown up to me and very distant. I never got to know him. And there had been a third brother, a ward, adopted, like me and around my age, but he was… sent away. My new father would not say anything on the subject; my new mother said only that the boy had proved difficult. Nox told me his younger brother had been evil, had caused trouble, had stolen, had killed one of the dogs. I did not believe him. I hated Nox from the very first.

(She stared into the fire and Tristram reminded her to eat her stew before it grew too cool. Alba smiled, began to eat, and he knew he should never have allowed her to begin this story. Tristram cleared his throat— I was thinking of calling in at the bookshop again and—*but Alba placed her bowl into the space on the rug between them and he knew she had to finish what she had begun.)*

I was very lonely and very unhappy. I thought the castle was anything but enchanted and I did not want to live in a forest. My eldest brother was always aloof and distant and rarely seen. And Nox…

My parents gave me a present. A locket. Very old and quite worn. A pelican on its face and the sun and the moon on the inside opposite their portraits.

(Tristram leaned forwards.)

A magic locket, they told me, a symbol of trust and love. I treasured it, very much, and it made me feel less alone, closer to my parents. For a while.

I never got chance to know my new mother very well. There was a fire. My adopted mother and eldest brother's rooms were in that wing. Nox raised the alarm. By the time anyone got there, the whole wing blazed. They helped my mother out. She was unharmed but the shock was too much for her.

My mother died within the week.

My eldest brother was nowhere to be found and, at first, we thought he had been in his rooms, that he had been killed by the fire.

(Tristram said nothing.)

But he had simply been away, somewhere out in the

forest or elsewhere. I never found out; there was never chance for him to tell his own story before the rumour spread: that the fire had started because of his negligence. My father was grief stricken, withdrawn when he was not furious over some thing or another. He sent my eldest brother away. Nox told me it was because the rumours were true, that it was a punishment. I was told by the estate manager that my brother would return when the rumours died down. They never did. They got worse and soon everyone seemed to believe he had been sent away because he had started the fire.

It was all too much for my father. In a terrible display of anger, he publicly disowned his eldest son and named Nox his sole heir.

I had not seen such a look of satisfaction on Nox's face. I've since grown too used to seeing it…

Father grew even more withdrawn between these bouts of fury. He drank, more and more he drank, Nox often watching each glassful drain away, his expression unreadable.

One evening, when Nox was off on some piece of family business on behalf of my father, my father came to dinner in a very drunken state. He ate nothing, drank more, until he asked me about the locket—did I still keep it close and treasure it? I admitted I did and he laughed. I said I thought it a wonderful token of love and better times. He laughed harder, although he agreed it was a symbol of better times.

He told me he had stolen the locket. A rival family had owned it. They were very prosperous, always outdoing him, and the source of their luck and luxury was the locket. So he stole it. They were ruined, he told me. And I had been given the locket as a gift not because he felt love for me but because the locket would attract a rich husband to me and bring more money to the family coffers.

I was twelve, Tristram. I dreamed of love and magic…

(Alba added wood to the fire. Tristram, wanting to spare her any more pain, offered to make tea. But Alba needed to finish:)

It was announced I was to be sent to boarding school, to

make a proper lady of me. I saw no need to hide my hatred of my adopted father, or my adopted brother, who watched me when he thought I was not looking. I wandered in the forest, counting off the days until I could go. For good, I vowed. Over those months, my adopted father grew ill. Weak, frail—everyone said it was the drink. But I watched Nox. I watched until I was certain and then I confronted him. He laughed at me. He tried to kiss me. But Nox never denied that he was poisoning his father.

Boarding school was a release. I vowed again I would never go back to the castle and I stayed at school during each vacation, sending away those come to collect me. And then my father died. I had not long turned fifteen. It was winter, a very cold one and the news I received was vague enough that I thought he had died of a chill but it was nothing of the sort. Accident was the official verdict: Nox was walking with his father around a lake on the estate. The older man slipped, the ice broke, he was too frail to help himself... Nox claimed to have tried to save his father and Nox was injured in the incident, a shard of ice impaling him in the leg and the upper groin. He never fully recovered.

Despite myself, I felt I had to return for the funeral. I took the locket—I still kept it with me, a reminder of sorts, or... I do not know why...

(She picked at her cold stew. At last, she set the bowl aside and leaned across the space between them, one hand reaching out, not touching Tristram but drawing patterns in the old carpet, runes and symbols that she smoothed away to begin again. Tristram did not move, hardly breathed. He could not look away.)

Nox greeted me with presents. Flowers on the morning of the funeral; flowers afterwards. He arranged dinners for us, cooked by his new chef and served by his new servants. I recognised not one face—everyone I had known was gone. I tried to avoid Nox, wanting to leave as soon as possible but there was always an excuse, just as there was always another present, another dinner. Until— One evening Nox got drunk. He admitted it all—the fire, poisoning his father, all of it. I told him he was mad. He told me he intended to marry me. I told him he was insane. I left at once. I ran from the castle. Somehow, I blundered to the edge of the lake. A thaw had reduced the ice to almost nothing. I had the locket with me— I threw it into the lake.

A search party found me. Captured me. I was taken back to the castle. I escaped the next day and the next. My room was locked and barred and there was no longer pretence that I was anything other than a prisoner. Nox demanded that I return the locket to him—for 'safe keeping'—and I had to admit I had thrown it away.

The lake was dredged. And then it was drained and the mud sifted. The locket was gone, gone completely.

(Alba pulled the hem of her skirt over her ankle.)

I managed to escape again. When, a few days later, they captured me, Nox forged the chain, link by link, and put it on me. I was poor compensation for the loss of the locket, he told me, but I was his, every bit as much as the locket was. He had no intention of letting me go.

Tristram sat in silence. The fire murmured, its observances forgotten and flames grown weak, glow adding only faint colour to Alba's face, a face in profile as she turned away from him, perhaps in the direction of the fireplace, perhaps elsewhere.

'I...' He cleared his throat. 'I had no idea.' The words little better than a mumble. 'I'm sorry. That's a terribly feeble thing to say but—'

'No. Thank you.' Alba nodded, rubbing her ankle as she spoke, attention fixed somewhere else, some other time or place, and Tristram felt questions grow dry and unspoken in his throat: *How does it feel, the chain? Is it heavy, always tight, are you always aware...?*

Standing and no true memory of doing so, Alba titling her head towards him, apparently waiting, the weight of unspoken words making his throat sore.

'I should go out, patrol, one last—'

'Yes. Of course.'

The fire was almost out.

'I won't be long. You'll be...?'

Alba nodded, fumbling for the blanket she used as a shawl.

The fire was almost out.

Passing behind her—close enough to almost brush against her, to feel the heat of her, close enough to feel her heart, almost, feel its beat—Tristram put more kindling in the grate, placing wood around it to create a chimney and draw new strength into the fire.

Tristram reached for his coat.

'Would you read to me?'

'I—uh—I'd like to, of course, but—'

'Yes, yes.' Alba pulled the blanket closer.

'I know the chain... But we should maintain watch.'

'Yes.'

So stuffy.

He heard Vivien laughing.

'When I return...'

'I might sleep, Tristram, I am quite tired—'

And you can be so frightfully boring, Tristram, so chivalrous, like your name.

I don't consider being responsible to be boring—

'Pardon?'

'Hm?'

The wind had scythed across Cardigan Bay, snapping the flags and pennants on the poles around Castle Point. Slate waters, granite clouds, shallow beach unable to offer any protection as the wind rolled another sputtering wave toward the promenade.

We should return to the hotel. Tristram had indicated the path over the mound, through the ruins of the castle.

Vivien had accused him of being stuffy again, turning towards the sea with her arms spread so the next gust had almost carried her away. He had felt the tall houses lining the terrace behind them squinting against the squall, watching Vivien with disapproval. No one else was out on the sea front, spindrift peppering the flagstones and the lamp posts swaying.

I'm sure your mother and sister will be waiting, he had begun.

All this talk of duty, it's so dreary.

She embraced the next gust of wind, laughing, saying again and again how dreary and stuffy he was.

Then why consent to marry me?

She spun and squeezed his face between her gloved hands.

Why, to see the look on your face, of course, my dearest.

Tristram swotted her away and her laughter was the wind coming in off the Irish Sea, battering the shore and the castle, Aberystwyth shrinking away to leave only waves and shingle and Vivien, laughing.

Aubrey says he would make a much better match for me, you know.

I don't like your friendship with that man. It isn't seemly. People will—

They will in any case, Vivien sneered.

That is no reason to encourage—

I encourage nothing. Her voice a gull, screaming. Her face was the wind digging claws into the sea and hurling it against the shore. *I told him to go away and join your little war*—and she flicked at the brass buttons of his khaki overcoat, the officer's pips on his shoulders—*instead of hiding away in his stuffy little office in his stuffy little reserved occupation. I told him I didn't care anything for him. And he laughed and laughed and told me that made him love me all the more.*

What a filthy, disgusting thing—

But we are *filthy and disgusting, trapped in this flesh, this—*

But that had been the curé talking, not—

I will never have children, Vivien had told him, *I will never let you touch me and I will never—*

'Pardon?'

The fire brushed the side of Alba's face. She was turned towards him but did not look at him. Flames spoke.

93

'Hm? Oh, nothing. I was…' Tristram laid the greatcoat across the chair. 'Doesn't matter.' He picked up one of the books, opening it as he sat on the rug opposite Alba, and began to read.

Each morning, a patrol. Each afternoon, on the cusp of evening, he set out again, greatcoat and boots, and snow working white through his beard and making cold kisses around the corner of each eye. It lay in deepening drifts, the snow, heaped up on the sides of carriageways and the larger footpaths so the city could keep moving, always restless and needing to flex itself. But little seemed to move during these morning and late afternoon wanderings; few people walked the pavements, cleared or thick with snow. He saw a dog on the corner of Irányi utca and Molnar utca. The dog followed a trail through the snow and paid Tristram no heed. No birds, that he heard, indeed very little sound other than the crunch of each footfall, the drone and grumble of motorcars and vans hushed, unwilling to break the pristine silence the snow gathered around itself. One afternoon, Tristram called by the second-hand bookshop, the few wooden crates outside containing bargain books huddled beneath a sheet of canvas. The bell rung, a fire banked and smouldering in a grate, warming a deserted shop. His skin tingled. Tristram browsed, putting back each novel he looked at, certain none of them would be suitable. He choose poetry, more or less at random, and a collection of short stories, before wavering, remembering Alba's delight with the first books he took her and not wanting to disappoint. Tristram snatched a novel from a shelf and got as far as the counter before doubt made him pause, read a little of this book, a little more of that one. At last taking four books to the counter. No one appeared. He waited. The fire crackled. He reached up and pinged the bell over the front door. No one, the note beside the till needing another few moments to catch his eye. He looked along the aisles and finally did as the note asked, writing down the titles he was taking, leaving a pile of change nearby.

The church with its onion dome craned back to catch falling snow in its mouth, the road deserted and, if there was traffic nearby, there was no hearing it. Tristram paused, a candle's shimmer dancing in the gap between the thin curtains across the half-moon window. Nothing moved around him. The snow held its breath. He crouched and leaned a little closer, pressing the books close to his chest. Alba crossed the space between the curtains, a cooking pot in her hand. A dull clink of metal on metal carried through the glass. He thought he could hear her singing, which was ridiculous because the sound could never carry. Tristram waited for another glimpse, snow and new books and the city of Pest forgotten, for a time, at least.

His own shouts woke him.

Shadows spun by the feeble glow from the window, grey into a deeper charcoal. Shapes, wavering with the pounding of his heart. Catching sight of the smouldering fire. Beginning to shiver. Startling as the shape closest to him resolved into Alba.

'You were dreaming.'

'Yes.'

Tristram managed to sit up part way. Alba tucked the blankets closer around him, her hands brushing against his shoulders, his hands, her skin luminous.

'I don't remember what I was dreaming of,' he mumbled before she could ask.

'Gone now,' Alba whispered.

He nodded.

Later, Tristram woke again. Night, dawn still out of reach. A smudge of shadow breathed beside him. He watched her sleep, relaxing slowly although his heart continued to run fast, making it difficult to reach over her and tuck the blankets she had dragged from the bed more snuggly around her. Tristram lay back and stared up at the dull light through the curtain, seeing a little of the window beneath its hem. Imagining a swirl of white a few seconds before it flittered beyond the glass, gone again.

The iron gate squeaked *hullo*.

Tristram sat in the wall niche. A black cat picked through the heaps of snow on the other side of the road, yellow jade flashing as it glanced towards Tristram, eyes narrowed against the reflection from the crest of the drift, alabaster bright against an overcast midday.

A crunch of footsteps.

Pretending not to hear, Tristram watched the cat, white cane making almost no sound as it searched for ice under the latest dusting.

'You should go in and keep her company.'

'I can't, father. I have to stay here and keep guard.' He made space on the ledge for the blind beggar to sit. Neither spoke and the road became motionless, even the black cat disappearing.

No sleeping. No will to leave yet. The dawn conjured a solid world out of shadows and the luminescence cast by the snow: a wall, a lamp post, a church. Breath misting the glass, window radiating cold against his hands on the ledge. Dreams clogging his thoughts.

'Tristram... Is something wrong?'

'No.'

Alba rubbed sleep from her eyes, sitting up. The bedstead creaked, the curtain hissing as it fell closed. Tristram stood at the foot of the bed.

'No, I, ah... I'm sorry. About leaving you, each morning.

Alba shook her head. Tristram ploughed on— 'I worry, you see. About you being scared, I mean. Alone, here, uncertain...'— before loosing thread of the words and grasping hold of the bed frame.

'I do not worry.' Alba pulled on her cardigan, arranging

the bedclothes around her. 'I know you will return, that you will come in and fix breakfast for us.'

He bit his lip, concentrating on his hands, the scrolls and leaves of iron beneath his palms.

'And the chain? It doesn't chafe? I mean, it's no longer as painful, isn't, ah...'

'It gives me no pain.' Alba smiled, burrowing a hand beneath blankets and quilt. 'It is slack, actually, quite slack. The slackest I remember it being.' She shrugged. 'Tristram, I think he might have gone. Nox might have simply given up.'

'You can't be sure.'

'No but the chain...' Alba laughed. 'The chain... Think, though, Tristram. If he has—'

'*If*, Alba—'

'If he has, I can travel.' She smiled and laughed, eyes wide at the thought. 'I can go anywhere. I could, there would be nothing to stop me, no one. I could— I could go back to Wales with you. We could leave the city and go to your home. That would be wonderful, do you not think, Tristram? To go to Wales together?'

'I— Oh—' Tristram caught sight of the window and stammered that he had lost track of the time. 'I really should go out on patrol,' he apologised and was out the door before Alba had chance to speak.

The city prowled and padded through drift and flurry, white hands and white eyes, its breath the mist that settled sometimes between falls of snow, or the blizzards that ran laughing through the streets late at night, upending dustbins and setting the dogs to howling. In the pauses and stretches of quiet between, in the mornings that glistened with ice and the glow of a dawn dressed in magpie's robes or an evening furled about itself, petals raven black, he walked the bounds of his protectorate, near blind to a coach lamp's glimmer or the sweep of a headlight, deaf to the crunch of overshoe on snow and sparing almost no thought for a dark shape on a corner, hat pulled low over his eyes.

To go to...

Several days had passed since then. The words brought a shortened temper, a tendency to impatience and sarcasm it was sometimes difficult to curb.

You're being dreary, Tristram.

Simply because I—

Yes, simply because. Now hurry up. I don't want to be kept waiting...

But there had been many happy times with Vivien, many of them. The first time they had met—he had just turned eighteen and Vivien was sixteen or so, a ball...

Snow fell, growing thicker and more slippery. Tristram frowned. Perhaps they had met at that garden party the summer before. But he asked her to dance at that ball. It had been fancy dress and he had gone in the guise of a character from Arthurian romance and Vivien had worn a Greek costume she had said was meant to be Diana but he had said looked like—

He thought, instead, of the first time their families had come together. That had been a garden party. He had noticed his father and Vivien's talking, thought nothing of it even when his father had come up to him later and suggested Tristram could do worse than court Vivien. A marriage made in heaven, had been his words. Tristram recalled the look on his father's face distinctly, although he had not been able to interpret it at the time. And Vivien had laughed at him when he repeated what his father had said—

A breeze picked at the snow, folding billows out of the air.

But the picnic just before the war, at Gorsedd Arberth, that had been—

'What, dearest Tristram?'

She stepped out between the folds of snow, white fading from her hat and the cape across her shoulders, flakes settling again, beginning to collect on her coat.

'I was only thinking—'

Vivien seemed quite solid and he almost reached out to take her hand.

'About how happy we will be?' Vivien caught snow in her cupped hand, peering at the flakes as they faded away in the light from the nearest streetlamp. 'Ours will be a perfect marriage.'

'Only if you give up Aubrey,' he snapped before he could restrain himself.

'Aubrey?' Vivien turned over her hand, snow flakes falling away. 'He's nothing. You know that, Tristram.'

'But—'

'I want only your love, Tristram.' She stepped closer, the air chill between them. 'You can love only me, Tristram. You know that, too?'

He wanted to argue but, with Vivien so close, there was nothing to do but agree because he knew it was true. So they stood there, and Tristram did not see that the snow was not settling on her shoulders but pausing only; that, if he looked closely enough, each flake could be seen, fluttering to the ground, through Vivien's apparently solid body.

Floor hard, despite blankets and bedding. Room cold, despite a smouldering fire, his greatcoat draped across his bed. Sleep fitful and splintered by dreams of lying awake when, on reflection, he must have been asleep.

Tristram turned on to his back and stared at the faint glimmer seeping under the curtains across the half-moon window.

Alba whimpered.

She turned, voice a mumble of breath and half-sounds that were not really words no matter what they sounded like.

Tristram faced the wall, pulling the coat up, over his ears to try and block out the sound, wishing Alba would be quiet, wishing she would stop dreaming, wishing he could sleep and not have to hear this, trying to pull the bedclothes up to block the sound and wishing. Wishing.

Bread and a small packet of salt in an oil cloth bag to keep dry in the snow, although no snow yet that morning, only mist. And vegetables and mushrooms in a string bag, soil still on their roots and caps, so snow fall could only save the bother of washing. No snow that morning, only mist, hanging, featureless. Tristram tried to think of shopping lists and errands, his thoughts unwilling to settle, caught on a breeze so they bobbed and turned about themselves, thoughts like snow flakes, he thought, and remembered a face, a voice, or a dream of a face and voice, boots slithering on compacted snow, slide taking him into the wall at the side of the pavement.

Tristram looked up. Mist almost fog. No snow. He had been sure it was snowing.

Tristram looked around. Haze filled the road, wiping features away from the buildings so they might be anywhere, any building, sight pulling his heart deep down into his stomach and fixing a gasp in his throat. But it was only that the mist made everything appear unfamiliar. He was not lost.

He had no idea where he was.

Turning. Slithering towards the nearest corner to interrogate the street names pinned to the wall. Almost falling as he dashed to another corner, needing to see names that meant something and finding, instead, Alba, alone and unsure where he was, Alba abandoned, Alba unprotected.

And Vivien.

He pushed the thought away but the image—a field, grass peeled away to show the bare earth beneath—refused to leave: Vivien alone in the midst of the field, the field piled with bare earth rutted and frost speckled, Vivien alone, Vivien—

A wind rose, pulling the mist and raising a flurry of snow. The snow turned and billowed. White wings. The train of a white robe. It turned and flapped and bent around itself, folding, hiding before it bent outwards, parting to let a dog step out, dog stopping to sit and peer at him, eyes narrowed and its head tilted to one side. Watching.

He ran, shopping bags confused, tangling with his legs as they tried sometimes to lead, sometimes to catch up with his haste. His anxiety drawing the clouds closer, closer in, mist fading away, leeching the day's light as it went, sucking out the colour. Day breathless, hollow, first flakes of snow caught in the slither and rush, spinning wildly.

Bags thumping against him. *Too late*, they rustled and mumbled, *too late, too late, too...*

Lustrous yellow gilded the curtains, shimmied through the crack between them, day gone to twilight, dark enough to be dusk come early. Tristram gasped, could not find breath. The flickering dance reminded him of the Hotel Ikrek and he could hear the crackle of flames eating, devouring.

The shopping thudded into the snow.

He shouldered open the door. Alba jumped, turning to stare as she shied back, candlelight painting shadows into a frown, a look of surprise into fear and back to surprise.

'Tristram?'

'You're fine? There's nothing—?'

'There's nothing— I'm—'

'I ran,' he gabbled, 'I've lost the shopping— The candles—'

'Whatever is wrong?' She crossed the room, hands trying to take hold of his arms, or shoulders, wanting to draw him into an embrace. 'Did you see something? Is something wrong? Tristram?'

'The candles, I saw—' He held her hand tightly as he searched for breath and words that made sense, the candles bending close, concern in each flame. 'Where did they come from?'

'A beggar woman—'

'You mustn't open the door.' It was impossible to find breath to speak, impossible to make his heart slow. The flames danced.

'I did not. She did not— I was already halfway up the stairs, on my way to the church—'

'Keep watch.' Nor could he let go of her hand. 'You

must always—'

'But I did. Tristram—' Alba managed to slip from his grasp, taking hold of his shoulder, stroking the side of his face with her other hand. 'What is wrong? Please, do not worry. I looked, both ways, before I continued up the steps, and then I paused again, and there was no one there. But when I turned to look back along the road, there she was, using her cane to—'

'Cane?'

'Yes. She was blind, a blind beggar woman, Tristram, like your friend, and she offered me all these candles. She told me she had no use for them anymore and asked if I wanted them.'

Tristram nodded. He pulled Alba into an embrace, brief and awkward. Promising to explain everything when he caught his breath, he stood back and watched the candles push away the twilight and plait gold through Alba's hair.

Outside, through the narrow chink in the thin curtains, white flashed across the windows and was gone.

Floor and the room cold, greatcoat and bedding taking the edge off both. The whimpering brought him awake, walking through the edges of his dream until it could catch his attention and make up sit up to listen.

Alba flailed against bedclothes and blankets, whimpers a mumble of breath and sounds not really words.

Cold worked through the rugs to chill his bare feet. Tristram padded closer, ignoring gooseflesh and the need to shiver, thinking he would add a little to the fire as her dream made Alba murmur and fret. He bent, almost thought better of it, and took her hand, cradling it between his own. Alba grew still, her dream ebbing and letting her settle deeper until she slept, simply slept.

Tristram knelt, keeping hold of Alba's hand, and kept vigil until dawn.

'Tell me—'

She frowned at the shirt in her lap, a slip of needles on the rug beside her, spools of thread near to hand.

'Hm?' He leaned over the stew pot, stirring and scenting the steam rising from what would be their evening meal. Another bay leaf, he thought. 'Tell you…?'

Alba turned over the shirt. New, for Tristram, that day, bought cheaply from a little second-hand shop because it missed several buttons and needed a little darning. He had seen it yesterday and Alba had made him go back that morning, unimpressed by his argument that two shirts were enough for anyone.

She found the needle she had been hunting for. 'Tell me something.'

'What?' Tristram stirred in another bay leaf.

'Anything.' She bent over her darning, turning the shirt towards the light from the fire and the candles, heavy clouds bringing another early twilight, afternoon more like late evening, day huddled near the fire, cosy in spite of fresh snow falling. 'Tell me anything, anything that comes to mind. Something about you.'

Another stir before putting the lid on the pot. Tristram stood, Alba holding up the shirt after another minute or so, inspecting her work before carrying on, looping thread through thread. He went to the window, parting the curtain just enough to see the church on the other side of the road. The only voices were flames: the fire in the grate, the candles, the stove. Enough silence to think the question had been forgotten, the moment passed, the road outside peaceful and unblemished.

'I knew a priest, during the war.'

He told her of the church and the curé. Of Ahriman, the bungling Creator of All. Of the curse of being flesh incarnated around a scrap of divine spark that was imprisoned far from its true home and its true god. The snow fell as he spoke. And the candles bent and flickered, plaiting more gold through Alba's hair, burnishing her frown of

103

concentration as she sewed on another button, or paused to listen to what the curé had said. The church across the road made no reaction and the snow fell, white over white, each crystal unique, it was said, each fitting against the next without jar or hitch.

The curtains fell back across the half-moon window, no amount of adjustment ever enough to get them to hang perfectly without of a gap of some kind.

'Do you believe him, Tristram?' Alba smoothed out the new shirt, button sound enough but the threads darning the holes did not match the rest of the cloth, mending obvious. She held his gaze. 'Is that how you think things are?'

Imperfections obvious to everyone.

'Don't you?' Tristram replied.

Only the flames spoke.

The cat oozed through the snow, an eel in black and white, eyes glimmering in the darkness as it wound around the side of a drift, head appearing over the ridge, watching him, unblinking. And the onion dome capping the bell tower shifted, straining to keep him in sight over the churchyard wall, lamp posts gone dark, windows black with thoughts of the dawn to come, catching a glimpse of him, holding on to it for a moment or two. And the rooftops, white wreathed, buildings no better than dozing, rousing to follow his path.

Sleep worse than fitful, Tristram had lain for hours, listening to Alba's soft breathing, staring at the ceiling or watching the changeless light coming through the curtain. No dreams when he had slept, none he remembered, only a mood that followed back into waking, would not leave him when he managed to sleep again, mood filling the basement room with suspicions and figments. Nothing definite, nothing he wanted to name. Clothes robbing him of the tiny bit of warmth his hard bed had given him, handle icy against his skin has he eased the door closed without waking Alba. Black and white cat pausing to watch as he climbed snow-clotted steps to the street.

The mood did not lift. It was a shadow-cat weaving between his legs as he walked. It was a breeze, whispering, whispering, the cold against his face, kisses that had an obsession, a cruel passion. The mood rose and took his hand, its skin pale and flawless. It took his hand and squeezed behind the knuckle of his index finger, finding the nerves and pinching before it relaxed to lie against his palm, not lifeless, simply dismissive, cold and flawless, a sculpture's dream of perfection. Anyone's dream—

A wind ran laughing along the length of the road, kicking loose snow into dervishes than spun and capered, white whorls, white billows. Vivien stepped out of the white, her robes trailing, caught by the wind, white against the white of air and ground, white the white of air and ground.

Tristram lurched back a step but could not escape.

A raven rode her shoulder, to leap with a clatter of wings, circling to rush through Vivien's body, almost too late for him to duck, wind of the bird's passage slapping him in the face as the raven perched on a nearby window ledge. The road was empty, only the bird and Tristram remained. He wondered if he was dreaming. But the bird settled its feathers and stared at him, eyes liquid black, catching the white of a snow bank, framing Tristram so he could almost see himself in their darkness.

The bird laughed.

Tristram fell back a step but could not escape.

The raven laughed again.

It was Vivien's laugh.

He walked until the city grew firm and flint edged, walked until the last of the night became the first of the new day, that day iron hard, impossible to doubt.

A fire crackled happily in the grate when he let himself back into the basement room, flames holding a conversation with the fat in the skillet, potatoes turning golden as porridge burbled to itself in the pot. Candles burned: either side of the hearth, on the little table in the corner, six or eight candles, their light more affable than the smoky flicker from the paraffin lamp could ever muster.

'What are you doing?'

Alba looked up from her cooking, smile faltering a little at his tone, his expression. He almost apologised.

'You can't waste wood like that, the fire's much too— And the candles—'

'We have plenty of wood.' Alba did not rise to his tone. She took the pans off the heat and nodded to the pile of wood in the scuttle beside the grate. 'The blind beggar woman brought more. She gave me more candles, too.'

'That's—' He could not see a way of backing down. 'It's not the point. And I fix breakfast.'

'Yes, except for today.' She turned back to the pots. No sign of ire or friction. He expected her to slam a spoon down. Or, rather, throw the food into the face of a servant. But there were no servants and Alba tasted the porridge, tested the firmness of the potatoes. The smell of fried onion and garlic wanted his attention.

'This is a thank you,' Alba was saying, 'for all the times you cook for me, all the mornings and evenings you go out to make sure we remain safe.'

When she told him to take off his wet boots and his coat, Tristram did as he was told. When Alba told him to sit, he did that, too, fire toasting one side of his face as he settled on the rug by the hearth.

'I remembered a story.' Alba handed him a plate and cutlery. 'When you told me about your curé, it reminded me of something and I could not recall it properly. Until this morning.' She smiled. 'How is breakfast?'

The last shred of resentment fell away. He sniffed the steam from the plate—peppers, garlic, onions, potatoes— could smell the porridge waiting to follow.

'Wonderful.'

'Good. Now, listen…'

This is from so long ago *(Alba told him)* that there was no Time, no Cosmos, only the One, only God, and God knew love.

God was all and everything, the One that was All. But God was also Two. A union of feminine and masculine, a light within darkness; a darkness within light. God was Two in One, the Everything that was Nothing, suffused with Wisdom and Beauty. A union of perfect love.

(She paused.)

This is difficult, because there was only the One but, little by little, the part of God that was Nothing began to dream and, in that dream, there was a voice. It came from the darkness and, in the dreams and in the thoughts that lingered afterwards, it came to seem that it was the Voice of the Darkness that whispered.

No love could be perfect enough, it whispered.

Well, the All that was Nothing did not listen. Yet the voice came from the darkness, faintly, always faintly, but it whispered: No love can be so perfect. Love is infinite, and infinitely varied, the voice murmured. With such multitude, there can be no certainty that *this* love is perfect, that some other love might not be greater in some way, that there might be another and that other might be the Perfect Love.

The All that was Nothing did not listen. It was All. It was many. It was One. There was no experience it did not experience. But the Nothing that was All listened as the Voice of the Darkness returned to whisper. The Nothing that was All found doubt, and that doubt settled around Wisdom and Beauty, that doubt made it harder to be loved and love Wisdom and Beauty in return. Wisdom is finite, the Darkness whispered, finite because it can never know Folly and so cannot encompass all there is to encompass. And Beauty, the Voice whispered, Beauty is timeless and only that which passes may truly be beautiful.

The Nothing that was All had heard enough and the voice that seemed to come from the Darkness fell silent. The Timeless and the Unmanifest—these things could not offer

Love, not Perfect Love nor Beauty. It was obvious to the Nothing that was All. There was no need for voices, whispering. It was obvious that things must change.

So that part of God that was Nothing and yet All turned over the fabric of space, causing Time to ooze forward into the gap created between here and there. And in that space where time passed, the material Cosmos condensed into being. Nothingness became Multiplicity, All splintering into Many. As the part of God that was Nothing and yet All acted, the dream voice, the voice that did not come from the darkness after all, this voice spoke within God and God, hearing, slipped. The old balance was shattered.

All of Wisdom, all of Beauty poured into the Cosmos. The Two in One became Two Apart, God fissuring into Severity and Mercy, into male and female divided. He, Severity, longed for the past; She, Mercy, remembered the breaking of Love and believed what was gone could never be reclaimed. The Two that had been One agreed only that the gulf between them was unbridgeable and that Unity was impossible. Yet, in each of us, a minuscule fraction of the lost One resides. And when there is love between humans, that union restores a fraction of the union before Time and Universe and the Two that were One come that fraction closer.

After finishing her story, Alba had pulled on her coat and boots and crossed the road to the iron gate, threading along the path to sit beneath the bell tower and its onion dome cap. Tristram brushed snow from the wall niche. The city grew silent, an aeroplane somewhere in the grey overhead circling in widening arcs until its engine grew too faint to hear. A black cat climbed on to the crest of the mound of snow in the opposite gutter. It sat, tail marking the end of a question. He had no idea what that question might be and, in any case, the blind beggar came around the corner before there was much chance to think over questions, or answers.

The beggar brushed the last of the snow from the niche and also sat.

Neither spoke, until Tristram frowned and cleared his throat.

'Do you know of a blind beggar woman?'

Smoked glasses tilted towards the ash sky.

'Yes, I think I know the person you mean.'

'Can she be trusted?'

'As much as anyone, I should imagine.'

'I saw—' Tristram noticed the cat had gone, a raven standing on its spot. He pretended not to notice. 'I saw a beggar woman at the train station and now she keeps appearing. I wonder... Is it suspicious, do you think?'

'I keep appearing.'

'Yes, but—'

'You should keep the lady company.' The beggar tilted his head: through the churchyard wall, towards Alba.

'She enjoys the solitude.' Tristram stared at the mound of snow. The raven had flown. 'I can't intrude.'

'Ah.'

Tristram was not going to speak on the matter again.

'You think otherwise?' he asked.

'No, not if the lady has told you this.'

'She... We've never spoken of it,' he admitted.

'Ah,' was all the blind beggar said.

Silence, stretching into another minute and not as comfortable as usual. Tristram waited, sure he could endure.

Tristram launched himself from the niche, pausing only a moment before opening the iron gate and stepping into the churchyard.

'It was only a few coppers.' He stood back and tried not to bite his lip.

The rug was threadbare in spots, and there were a few stains, faded almost to the point where they were only just discernible amongst the pattern.

'I thought, well, it does get cold in here and in the mornings...'

Snow pressed against the window, trying to look inside.

'It was only a few coppers,' Tristram repeated, excuse enough to roll up the rug and take it back to the shop, hope to get a coin or two in return.

'Under the window.' Alba pointed.

'I was thinking—'

'But you have to sleep on the floor and this room gets cold.' She dragged the rug into place.

'But, I was thinking,' he stammered.

'A present for the house.' Alba straightened the rug and stood back, smiling. 'I like it. Thank you. Our house thanks you, Tristram.'

He looked away and mumbled something or other.

'Perhaps I should look for a job,' Alba said later, as they ate breakfast.

'We still have money.'

'You are very careful, Tristram.' She nodded towards the new rug. 'Very good at finding bargains.' When he tried to deflect her words, she leaned over and clasped his wrist. 'I mean it. I am impressed.'

'Oh. Well.' It was tempting to leave it at that but Tristram explained, 'My family were actually quite strapped—death duties, poor investments and the like. Vivien used to tease me.' He swallowed, porridge suddenly bitter in his mouth. 'She teased my *economy*.'

They ate in silence.

Alba put aside her bowl.

'I remembered a story, another story,' she told him, waiting until he nodded. 'Another story about your locket...'

There were two lockets, identical to most eyes. One made by the master and the other by the apprentice. Although identical to most eyes, there were some who could see one was finer than the other and master and apprentice came to argue over who had created the better locket, the most perfect, the most beautiful. The apprentice accused the master of trying to steal credit and passing off the master's inferior work as the apprentice's own. And the master said same about the apprentice.

Their argument became heated. Their argument caught fire. The workshop burst into flames. And *(Alba held up a finger)* one of the lockets was utterly destroyed.

(Tristram asked which one and Alba smiled.)

No one knows. With nothing to compare it to, the surviving locket is perfect in itself but, all the same, it might be truly perfect, or it might only appear so, its flaws no longer apparent without its twin to hold it against.

Some say it brings good fortune. That fortune never lasts. Some offer it as a token of love. That love is always forlorn. And some say the locket is actually a test that no one has yet passed. Pass and you receive your heart's bounty and want for nothing but no one knows what the test is, nor how to take it.

But *(Alba stressed)* once lost, the locket cannot be regained. Everyone agrees on that.

A shadow was fixed to the edge of the window.

Clouds pressed closer, bringing promises of more snow that evening. Tristram paused as he trudged around the corner of the church, a bundle of firewood on his shoulder. An aeroplane engine droned again, circling lower. He frowned. The shadow did not move. A moment later, he glanced back but the blind beggar, there a moment earlier, was gone.

The shadow moved.

'Oi.'

The shadow became the landlord, beckoning.

Tristram tried not to look towards the church, hoping Alba was still sitting in the churchyard.

'Oi, you.' The landlord jerked a thumb towards the window. 'Very cosy, that. Yers. I should charge more rent, shoul'n't I? You've made it very 'omely, you 'ave.'

'Thank you.'

'Got a woman's touch it's got. You got a bint?'

Tristram set the cord of wood down and stared at the landlord, careful not to blink or look aside. 'No. Why? Do you know someone I should meet?'

'Cheeky git. You got a bird in there, ain'tcha?' The landlord poked Tristram in the ribs.

Tristram stood very still. 'You said you didn't care who I lived with.'

'No I never—'

'*Don't care 'oo you live wiv*— Those were your exact words.'

'I never—' The landlord looked down the road. 'I don' want that fackin' tramp in there, right? That blind bleeder. You gerrit?' He slithered and slipped away in the direction of the tavern where Tristram had first found him. 'And don' make me come back 'ere to bleedin' remind you, right?'

The aeroplane's drone filled the silence.

Alba looked up from her book.

'Vivien—'

'Yes?' Tristram was darning one of his socks. The cord of wood lay beside the hearth, dinner things put away. Snow whispered outside, curtains drawn as tightly as they may and the door locked. 'Vivien?'

'I was…' Alba looked down at the book in her lap. 'In the War, it must have been— A great comfort. Knowing she was waiting. For you. Do you think?'

Wherever she had been intending to take her question, this was not it. Tristram held his mending up to the firelight. 'I had her with me.'

Alba leaned forward. 'She was there?'

'At least in dreams.' He concentrated on rethreading the needle.

'Please' Alba prompted him a second time. 'Please, go on.'

112

'I wasn't...' He looked at the flames but they told him to continue now he had started. 'When I closed my eyes, Vivien was there. And she was there when I looked across the battlefield. Pale and perfect and untouched by any of it.'

'It?'

'The filth, the savagery.' He bent over his mending. 'The fear most of all. None of it touched her.' He put the work aside. 'She was so perfect and I was unclean, sullied by what I had done and seen. But it wasn't... it wasn't that. It was my heart. My heart was too weak,' he whispered. 'I lost faith. I...'

'Tristram...'

He held up a hand. The fire was beginning to dwindle, drawing light and heat into itself so the room grew colder.

'I saw her. Close to, I mean. She came to me.' Tristram took kindling and began resurrecting the fire. 'I thought she did, once.' He put water in the kettle, began making tea. Better to leave the story untold and let admission be enough.

Tristram set the tea pot on the hearth.

Alba remained silent. Waiting. Tristram searched for a change of topic and sighed.

'We had to go out into no-man's-land.' He stopped fussing with the tea cups and sat opposite Alba.

'We came under fire and my sergeant and I were separated from the other men. The firing grew heavier—the Germans brought up another machine gun—so we tried to find cover in a shell hole.'

Alba poured him a cup of tea. 'What happened?'

'Our lines returned fire and a mortar hit the machine gunners. I told my sergeant to stay down but he wanted to make a dash for it.' He looked into the steam rising from the cup. 'A sniper killed him the moment he stood up. His body knocked me back into the crater, so the sniper's next shot went wide.'

Tristram had lain under the other man's body for an hour or more, listening as the fighting grew sporadic. Cold, cramped, he waited until the skirmish petered out. Finally, Tristram heaved the dead man's body aside.

'Another bullet hit my sergeant's body, almost the instant it moved: the sniper was still waiting. It was hours until nightfall and even cover of darkness was no guarantee I would escape. I was exhausted. There seemed no hope of life, or that there could be anything other than mud and killing and the sheer disgust of it all.' Tristram put aside the cup, tea untasted.

'So,' he continued, 'so I tried to stand up and give that sniper a clear shot. My sergeant pulled me back into the shell hole and the shot missed me.'

'He was not dead?'

He was. Yet the sergeant's grip on Tristram had been unshakable.

She wants to see you, the sergeant had hissed, pointing deep into no-man's-land. At first, Tristram thought he saw a white bird skimming over the devastation but it was Vivien, hair a black thunderhead surrounding her, pale robes fluttering with the speed of her flight.

Both sides opened fire. Each bullet and shell faltered and dropped to earth. Untouched, Vivien stood over him. Her hand slashed the air and silence fell across the battlefield. The sun turned to lead, its dull light seeping through rents in the clouds.

'Aren't I enough for you?'

Tristram stumbled and fell backwards.

'Isn't living for me reason enough to keep living?'

Vivien towered over him, terrible and ice white.

Tristram squirmed, trying not to look at her as he admitted he saw nothing any more other than the fighting and the trenches, this wasteland all there was. 'Even when I close my eyes,' Tristram stammered, 'all I see is this. I don't see you any more.'

A white fire blazed, Vivien so bright the sight of her was painful.

'You know I have a life for you, waiting for your return.'

It was hopeless, yet Tristram wriggled out of the dead sergeant's grip and began to run.

The sound of the rifle was low and drawn out, a tortured growl. Tristram looked back and saw smoke ooze, flames unfurl from a muzzle, sniper's bullet creeping towards him, glimmering in Vivien's unforgiving glare.

Slowly, slowly. Time enough to dodge. But the bullet, calm and inexorable, turned to follow him and Tristram had known he would never outrun it.

'She was right to be angry with me,' he told Alba. Tristram wiped a hand across his mouth. 'She offered me a life, one bigger than I could hope for without her. I lost faith. How… ungrateful.'

A few embers remained in the hearth.

'It wasn't until then that I truly understood that we were linked, Vivien and I. More strongly than by engagement rings.' Alba was silent, her expression quite unreadable. All the same, Tristram searched for some word of apology, some way of minimising everything he had said.

She reached forward, taking his hand and squeezing, holding on to it as she asked about the sniper's last bullet.

'I woke up in hospital.' Tristram slipped his hand free and pointed to a scar just visible beneath the stubble above his temple. 'A crease. Bad, I suppose, but only a crease.' He busied over the hearth, trying to stop his hands shaking. 'I have no memory of being rescued. Only of Vivien's anger.'

Alba drew her knees up to her chest, tucking the hem of her skirt around her feet. 'I can see why you love her.'

'Yes.' He spoke without thought. 'Loved.'

'Loved?'

Tristram sat and, finding the tea cup cold, had no choice but to set it aside. 'Yes. She— Vivien died, of the 'flu, in 1919.'

The droning of aeroplanes was beginning to bother him. Each time he went out, something was circling overhead beyond the clouds.

A street dog stopped its amble to look up, too. A crow settled on frost-speckled branches and craned its head. An alley cat, a jackdaw, a magpie looked into a sky painted with cloud, sky made pale by the sunrise, a sky that droned. A hornet circling over the city of Pest.

Black wings beat the air. A raven settled on the wall beside him. Tristram looked away.

A glimpse, crossing the mouth of the junction ahead. Gone as he looked up. Black. And white. And the drone of an engine.

Tristram dashed to the corner in time to see black at a turning along the next road. Black of boot and roof. Just, just possibly a flicker of whitewall, snow beginning to fall again, flakes dampening sound so he could only guess at the rumble of the limousine's engine.

From this corner to that turning. From that turning to the next corner, road ahead straight. Not sure he saw anything and running on. Almost falling and keeping up the chase. A shadow. A gyre of snow. An engine, somewhere, muttering, muttering. Tristram panting, legs burning and heavy. Forcing himself on. Pausing, corner after turning.

And there it was.

He almost fell, shock stiff-arming him hard in the ribs. A black and white limousine, gliding beside the Danube flowing in the opposite direction. *The* limousine, he was sure, picking up the chase again, unsure what he was going to do when he caught up, only certain he had to. The car slowed at a crossing. It was hard to get any more speed out of his legs but he was closer, the car slowly pulling away from the crossing and Tristram no more than an arm's length away as the car paused for another junction, closer as the car turned, swinging up the ramp and on to Széchenyi bridge, his hand almost on the rear wing, narrow lanes of cleared snow and the weight of traffic making the limousine crawl across the bridge, over the slow moving Danube.

Tristram clutched a wall, legs on the point of giving way. A lorry hid the black and white car, limousine halfway, almost into Buda.

A sludge of snow and ice dragged against the bank. The

spires and towers of Buda squatted on their hillsides, hooded and watchful. Tristram looked at the footpath, shuffling back a step so there could be no doubt he was off the bridge and on the shores of Pest. Still in Pest.

The limousine was gone.

He glanced up, looking a second time, searching across roofs and towers, limousine forgotten as he looked for evidence of the vision, unable to be certain he had not just seen Vivien, towering over road and bridge, barring his way into Buda.

'Watch,' he said, gripping the blind beggar's hands. 'You must keep watch.'

Her voice woke him.

It had been a difficult day, a harder evening as he had no reason to avoid Alba. She asked what was wrong. When he snapped at her, she had simply asked him again, forcing him to mumble that it was nothing, nothing, and, hating himself for lying, he had sat in sour silence, trying to avoid her gaze until she had given a stiff apology and gone early to bed. He had tried to think of ways of telling her what he had seen. The black and white limousine that, as he sat in the basement room, beside the hearth fire, he could not be entirely sure was Nox's car, could not be sure the vehicle rolling across Széchenyi bridge was even black and white. Everything had been so confused. And the vision—Vivien grown to impossible, terrifying size. It sounded insane. So he had kept his silence and, hating himself for that cowardice, was sure he would never sleep.

Her voice woke him.

'In the smoke,' she mumbled.

'Shhh.' He took her hand. Alba twisted in her sleep. The dream would not let her go, although she raised her other hand and pointed.

'Dark, in the smoke.'

Tristram gently eased her arm back to her side, hushing her again.

'In the smoke,' Alba mumbled, beginning to squirm. 'Dark. Dark man. In the...'

Tristram could not move.

'Dark man,' Alba murmured. 'Coming... close... Dark.'

The chain offered no reaction.

He watched for a sign, any indication it was growing tighter. If Alba noticed his scrutiny, he scrambled to find lies and excuses. Because it was only suspicion, he reminded himself. No sense in alarming her on the basis of a chase through the snow, or a dream. So he watched and pretended he was doing nothing of the sort.

Alba watched him in turn and the atmosphere in the room changed.

Tristram set out earlier in the mornings. Moving slowly and lingering at each corner, always looking behind him, always expecting the limousine to steal into view. Because it might. As he looked away, or turned a corner, that could be when Nox chose to appear, in a moment's inattention, an instant's distraction. Provisions unbought for the fear that, during the minutes it took to choose and pay, the limousine might already have vanished, unheeded. Patrols growing longer, just in case in the next second, the seconds after that, Nox might... because Nox could, could easily... Just when Tristram was not looking.

So he returned later, long after breakfast, without explanation or provisions. Alba watched and the atmosphere between them sharpened.

Even so, Tristram set out each afternoon. To walk slowly even if haste tugged at his hand and urged him to run, street to street, without pause, without thought, because there was a chance, slim or great, there was no knowing, but a chance that on the next street or the corner after that, there would be the limousine and there would be Nox and, unless Tristram hurried, faster, he might miss car and man—

But he held himself stiffly, paid deliberate attention to each footstep and each place he went. He had made a commitment and panicking would not help. So he held himself more stiffly and pushed down on the panic.

Alba saw his stiffness and replied in kind. And the atmosphere changed.

Tristram heard Vivien's voice as he patrolled. He heard the drone of engines, near and far. And, in between, Vivien spoke. He ignored her, as best he could, reminding himself this was a commitment to offer aid and protection, purely and simply that and nothing more.

He heard Vivien's voice and he told her to shut up.

Vivien mocked, disdain become a squall of snow beating the air around him as he ran, snow turning black—crows' wings, jackdaws'—turning black and white—flights of magpies growing paws, claws cutting into the snow, cats, black and white, dogs, snarling, snapping back, snapping white, snapping black, black as Nox's eyes, black as darkness, as ravens, birds mobbing him as he ran until her hand found his, cold and pale and too perfect to exist in this fallen world, her voice finding him through the clatter of wings and the endless, endless droning of engines and tyres crunching over snow turning black again, Vivien the only flash of pure white to be found in this chaos. Like marble. Like a flame.

I'll take you to safety, she told him. *My sweet*—

'— pissed, at this time ov day.'

The finger jabbed him in the chest again.

'You berra wotch tha'. End up not payin' the rent this way, yo' know, an' I ain' 'avin' tha'.'

The landlord peered at him, dog-end glued to his bottom lip.

'What do you want?'

They were near to Szerb utca, almost home. No sign of Vivien.

'What do you want?' Tristram asked again.

'I woz jus' lookin' in yer winda—'

Tristram stiffened, stopping himself grabbing the other man's collar at the very last moment.

'An' 'e's right. Yo' lied, dintcha? Yo' gorra bint—'

'You—' Biting off the first sentence that came to mind, Tristram said carefully, 'You have evidence, do you, that I'm living with someone? You '

The landlord drew breath. Let it out again. 'It looks neat an' tidy,' was the best he could manage.

Tristram tried not to stare at the steps to the basement door, pushed away any thought of Alba, assuring himself she must—*must*—be across the road in the churchyard, that was why the landlord had seen—

'Someone has lied to you.'

'Yo' ain' go'—'

'You've been lied to.'

''E din' look th' type. Posh 'e was, dead posh. Woss a posh bloke doin', lyin' to the likes o' me abou' th' like's o' you havin' a bint livin' witcha if yo' ain' gorra a bint livin' witcha, uh?' The landlord smiled at this tortuous chain of logic. 'I won' ask for much more rent, eh? Yo' jus' let me see 'er for m'sel', eh? 'E said she were a bit special.'

'It's not safe.'

Alba was in the churchyard, although it was the last place he looked, after checking the basement room and walking the streets around Szerb, looking for signs of limousine or Nox.

'You must leave.'

Alba stared, uncomprehending. 'What do you mean?'

'Nox. He's close.'

'The chain.' She leaned forward on the bench, lifting the hem of her skirt. 'No pain. No tightness. Nothing, Tristram.'

'I've seen… things.' He paced, impatient with this need to explain. 'Signs,' he snapped.

'There is no need for alarm, Tristram.' Alba reached out, trying to halt him. He backed away.

'The landlord— Someone—' He clenched his fists.

120

'There's no time to debate. I know.'

Alba stood. 'Please, Tristram, do not shout. Please, sit. Tell me—'

'You have to leave. Now. Right now, before it's too late. Right away.'

'Very well.' She gathered her book, tucking her shawl more tightly around her as she spoke. 'Very well, if that is what you say, then we must go—'

'Alone.' Tristram put a hand across his mouth, admission taking him by surprise. 'You have to go alone,' he pressed on. 'I— I can't protect you. Not—' Tristram looked up, searching for sign of white against grey snow cloud. 'I can't any longer.'

The book fell from her hand. 'But...'

Tristram spun, began walking. There was nothing more he could say.

The blind beggar was waiting as he rushed from the churchyard, iron gate squealing.

'You know.' The beggar tried to hold him. Tristram pushed the beggar away.

'You know,' the blind beggar called after him.

Tristram walked faster.

'You've seen him, yes?' the beggar shouted. 'You've seen him?'

Ten minutes at most.

Tristram had stopped walking. The day crowded close around him, jostling, yelling in his face, Vivien's voice amongst the din. Snow against his face. He had ignored that, and the wind that was beginning to find strength enough to kick rime from the top of the drifts. The day jostled and pushed him. It slapped him across the back of the head, Vivien yelling at him, at the day, and her voice no longer quite cutting through. Tristram had turned back. Running.

Ten minutes at most. He had been away from the basement room and the churchyard and the tall spire with its onion domed head for no longer than that.

Alba was gone.

Snow rose up, dressing itself in overcoats and scarves, in a dozen kinds of shawl, two dozen different sorts of faces. It walked ahead of Tristram. Or it peered, head bowed, from half-open doorways, its face glimpsed at the entrances to alleyways and side roads, flittering at the corner of his eye. And always at the moment he was most distracted, most distraught. Always wearing a pale face and hair spun from morning gold. Tens of faces, scattered amongst crowds of hundreds, or in the back seats of motorcars, on the flat beds of drays and lorries that barked and snapped as they swerved violently through the crowds. Each face made his breath hitch, his heart lurch. But none of them was Alba.

Despair laid a cool hand against his face, wiping away the sweat beginning to freeze in his short hair. Whispering.

It used Vivien's voice.

Tristram staggered down the length of another road. Stopping to turn, peer over his shoulder. In case... In case...

Faces pale as mist. Faces of snow, powdered and delicate. None of them Alba, although the next one might be. Or he might already have missed her, somewhere. He might, he said and despair nodded, gripping his hand more tightly, trying to drag him from here, back to the basement room or the churchyard. It does not matter, despair whispered. Tristram turned away. A flutter of midnight, black touched with purple's blush. Obsidian eyes and a beak of jet. The carrion crow spoke once, voice hoarse, words as dark as its wings, before it hopped away, wings smoke caught on the wind.

It settled a little further down the road and stared at him, waiting.

Tristram could not make himself move. The crow snapped its beak.

First step a stumble and the second no more certain, Tristram followed the crow. Along an alley. To a yard enclosed on four sides, snow piled deep as his waist so he had to wade and flounder across its length. Carrion crow growing impatient. Crow more sarcastic. He called for it to wait. More midnight blue than black, the bird soared over the roofs, leaving him, sweating and swearing, numbed with snow melt.

When he fell out of the alley mouth on the other side of the yard, the crow laughed and beckoned him on with an imperious sweep of a wing.

Tristram heaved to his feet. An alley turned into another courtyard, into another alley, a lane that turned right angles about itself. Tristram tried not to loose sight of the carrion crow; but it pulled ahead. Little strength left, he threw himself forward, black ice under the new-fall snatching his balance. Tristram windmilled into a wall, to rebound, wheel and stumble through a narrow archway. To fall.

A flutter of wings, midnight blue passing across his face.

'My dearest friend.'

To fall into waiting arms.

It was Voit.

'You have not injured yourself, I trust, dearest Tristram?' Voit smiled with concern.

Voit. In midnight overcoat. Voit. A silk muffler sheened by wear. Voit. High forehead bare, oblivious to cold and falling snow as he tried to steady Tristram. Tristram ready to collapse, unable to find his balance. Unable to understand.

Voit.

'You died.' The two words robbed him of the last of his breath, Voit struggling to keep him upright. Tristram strained to breathe. 'You— I thought you died. No word, nothing, nothing...'

'A misunderstanding.' Voit adjusted his grip on Tristram's arms, guiding them both through the snow. 'It was necessary. You must believe me, my friend, you simply must.'

'But—' The lane made a turning, a second low arch leading towards some sort of wide courtyard beyond. A motorcar idled, exhaust weaving through falling snow, bobbing as it tried and failed, tried and failed to catch even one drifting flake. Tristram straightened, clutching Voit's arm. 'He's here. *Nox*.'

'Indeed?' Voit raised an eyebrow.

'My landlord—' An aircraft moved unseen, rooftop to rooftop, watching. Tristram halted, staring at the little patch of courtyard the arch was willing to reveal to him. The motorcar idled beyond the corner of the nearest building, exhaust smoke billowing to pause and watch as they came closer. 'My landlord said,' Tristram hissed.

'This is concerning,' Voit whispered, still holding on to Tristram. 'Although, your landlord is not especially trustworthy.' He nudged Tristram forward again. 'Don't you agree?'

'I—' The car was black, a saloon not a limousine. Tristram began to relax until the implication of Voit's statement turned over in his stomach. 'You know him?'

'No.' Voit waved to someone in the car. Wings fluttered. 'Although I have met him, of course, I should not say anything other than 'acquainted', if you will allow the distinction. A base fellow.'

Wings fluttered, black against the snow. The engine idled. A door opened. Voices, male, female. Car rocking.

'In any event,' Voit began.

A voice, raised in anger and fear. And someone climbing out of the car. A nondescript man, anonymous in any crowd but triggering a memory—*the reek of sweat and beer... you fat fuckin' fucker*—recognition unhinging Tristram's mouth, all thought suspended by the effort of trying to understand why this man was here.

'In any event,' Voit began again, 'it's only proper that we make our goodbyes. Mátyás, if you would be so kind?'

The man grinned as he leaned back into the car. Wings rag-flapping against the air, jet this time, not purple-touched midnight, producing a raven out of thin air, bird perching on the top of snow piled at the side of the courtyard. A dog

124

barked in the near distance. The raven made no sound, only watched Tristram watch as the man who had assaulted Kata leaned into the saloon, car rocking, a voice, a woman's voice, yelling, insisting.

Alba.

Mátyás had her arm twisted behind her back. Another man, a port wine stain spilled down half his face, also emerged from the idling car, holding on to Alba's wrist so she could hardly move. Only struggle. Only yell. Only fall silent when she saw Tristram.

Only to begin struggling against Mátyás.

'Run, Tristram, run.' Alba managed to pull her hand free and smack Port-wine across the ear. He grunted and wrenched her hair, regaining hold of her arm as she flinched.

'Not too fat this one, eh, Mr Voit?' Mátyás grinned. Alba managed to kick him in the shin. Mátyás grinned and winked at Tristram.

'I'll—' Tristram could not move.

'I would advise against a rescue, dear Tristram.' Voit raised a cautionary finger as Alba screamed for Tristram to run while he had chance. Port-wine slapped a hand over her mouth. Mátyás wrestled Alba into a close embrace, his attention fixed on Tristram.

Tristram took a step.

The raven cawed loudly. Tristram looked it in the eye.

'Shut up,' Voit snapped at the bird, 'and fuck off, you're not needed.'

The bird cawed more harshly, eyes fixed on Tristram. Tristram caught between the bird and the events around him: Alba struggling, managing to plead with him despite the efforts of Mátyás and Port-wine to shut her up, the engine idling, Voit beside him. The raven raised its wings.

In warning.

He could do nothing. He took a step forward.

'Oh dear,' Voit sighed, tugging something from the pocket of the midnight overcoat.

The pain was too great to feel at first, momentum

pitching his head forward, the rest of his body following as his knees gave way.

Mátyás chortled.

'My apologies, my dear friend.' Voit's face refused to come into focus. A white gauze fluttered behind him as he leaned over Tristram, the wings of some terrible bird, paler than ash, more unforgiving than any arctic waste and colder, too. 'I trust you will forgive me in time but—' Voit gestured with a magician's wand— 'I have the prize I have so long wished for.' Alba screamed. Again, Tristram remembered: Alba was screaming again, because she had screamed when Voit first hit him with the wand—not a wand, he dimly accepted, just a section of lead pipe. Tristram blinked slowly, the pain stirring, beginning to force long fingers through the crack his skull.

'Well, I see no good to be had in prolonging this.' Voit sighed, the raven cawing loudly so he had to yell at it to fucking well shut up before he could order Mátyás and Portwine back into the car.

'I do not think we will meet again, dear Tristram.' Voit raised the lead pipe. 'I will live with that loss.'

Tristram blacked out and there was nothing, not even the fluttering of white wings, until he felt hands cradling his head. Only one eye could open for some reason and that found a face framed by white hair, smoked glasses hiding eyes, face not quite a man's, face not quite a woman's.

'Try not to move.'

Tristram managed not to nod.

The blind beggar's fingers moved. Tristram hissed with pain.

'This is quite serious.'

Tristram nodded.

And then he passed out again.

III
CITRINAS

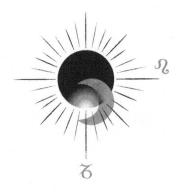

GRADUALLY, VOICES FOUND him. A man and a women. Or two women. It was hard to tell, the voices muffled by rags of darkness that also clouded vision but did little to blunt the rise and fall of the pain coiled around his head. He planned to hold on to the pain, because that seemed vivid, concrete, and it might take him somewhere where the darkness was less, or different. Something like that. Before he could decide, the pain slipped away, taking the voices with it and leaving him with— Nothing.

It was sunlight. He recognised it eventually, after watching it without understanding what he saw or that he was awake at all. And the thing rising up beside him: that was a wall, flaxen brightness reaching across him to spread itself up along it, towards the ceiling. Sunlight. And the softness pinning him down yet not letting him fall, as the pain rose and fell, that thing—

A bed.

The words fell away and he followed.

Rain woke him from a memory. Daylight, grey-streaked and cold against his face. He listened to the gutters, the trickling of water tripping over itself. He listened to the rain, tapping, tapping. And the memory remained as he opened his eyes: Alba, screaming. And Mátyás. And Voit.

The rain grew quiet, unable to help him decide how the memory might end.

The rain was waiting for him when he next woke. It beat against the window above his head. It throbbed and, in this space between sleep and wakefulness, it might have been an aeroplane crossing low over the city. The sound was gone, or never was, and he felt himself sinking, wanting to sink, willing to drown in sleep.

There was a shape at the end of the bed.

Better to let it go, better to sleep. But something called him back to wakefulness, awake enough to see smoked glasses and a mop of white hair.

'Ah, good. Almost awake. Next time, yes?' The figure leaned a little closer, features smudged by rain streaming down the window pane, light fumbling over a full lip, a brow that looked angular amongst the shadows.

'I am Tiresias.'

Tristram managed to nod. And then sleep returned.

Tall and aloof, the house stood on the edge of the Jewish quarter, guarded on three sides by walled garden and outbuildings, the one face it presented to the bustle of people hurrying along Kazinczy utca quite unremarkable, quite forgettable. People took no notice of this tall house and if the house took any notice of each passer-by, it showed no sign of it.

Tristram levered himself up to look out the window: the garden, filled with herbs and vegetables, vines crawling up the sides of the outbuildings and the high wall that stewarded it all; beyond that: roofs and buildings damp and almost as grey as the clouds and the rain falling from them. The snow faded under the downpour, much as the bruises on his shoulder and back faded, the wound on his forehead knitting together. Yet the snow clung on, here, there, and he still found movement difficult, grabbing door handles and banister rails for support as he shuffled from the room and climbed, one stair at a time, down to the kitchen at the front of the house, two floors below. The stiffness in his muscles was less, and the waves of dizzying nausea came infrequently, some days not at all. Still the climb down two flights exhausted him, leaving no choice but to sit in the kitchen and watch the people hurrying past along Kazinczy utca, each busy with their days and their lives as the rain drummed and slithered against the window.

A tailor's dummy loitered in the hallway outside his room. Another watched from the head of the flight of stairs leading up to the floor above; a third stood aside as he made his way down to the floor below. Two dummies waited half-way along the first floor hallway, one with a head of *papier mâché*, eyes indicated by streaks of paint, the other with a wooden arm attached by a musculature of leather. As always, it pointed towards the kitchen.

When Tristram asked, Tiresias had no idea where the dummies had come from or why they continued to be in the house. 'I don't see them any more,' the blind beggar had said, without irony: Tiresias simply accepted them and, having accepted, ceased to be aware of the dummies.

'I had them made.' Rózsa glanced up from her mending. Tiresias seemed not to notice her, either: a small woman, not exactly plump if certainly not slim, face ruddy and worn by work, a life that had not been cushioned by privilege and class. Not that being born into a higher class guaranteed ease and comfort, Tristram knew. He tried not to think of Alba.

The blind beggar took a dun brown overcoat from the row of hooks near the iron range before opening the door to the entrance hall. A moment later, the front door closed with a snick of the latch and Tiresias crossed in front of the rain-streaked window.

'You...' Tristram craned to watch until the beggar was no longer visible. 'You're a seamstress?'

Rózsa tied off the thread and handed the mended shirt to Tristram. 'I can sew, if that's what you mean.' Washing stood on wooden airers around the range, the kitchen warm and humid, fragrant with the herbs strung across the ceiling, the flasks filled with many colours, each fermenting merrily in the heat, bubbles crawling around the glass air traps fitted into each one. To pop, pop, pop.

Only Tiresias and Rózsa , the housekeeper, lived in the tall house. Unless the dummies counted. Tristram spent much of each day sitting beside the kitchen window as Rózsa went about her chores, cooking and washing, making bread or tending to the fermenting brews of tea and fruit and vegetables. Tiresias spent most of each day out of the house. Begging, Tristram presumed, as if that were a profession like being a book-keeper or an articles clerk, and Tristram imagined Tiresias walking to an office in the niche of the churchyard wall each day, there to—

'Here.' Rózsa held out a cup of tea, freshly brewed from the herbs hanging from the ceiling, or stored in jars along the walls. 'Take this, too.' A bottle, glass blue and impossible to see through, and a spoon to administer the dose. Tristram swallowed the tincture and handed back the bottle.

The door to the stairs creaked open and the white chicken stalked into the room. It paused, staring at Tristram. He tried not to stare back. The bird got bored quickly, flapping its wings madly to gain enough lift to reach the edge of the kitchen table, where it settled and went to sleep.

He knew Rózsa was watching him as he watched the chicken. But Tristram concentrated on drinking his tea and said nothing.

He asked Tiresias for something to help with sleep.

They were sitting at the kitchen table, dinner a thick vegetable stew, seasoned with caraway and chervil and pepper. Tristram had long since forgotten to miss meat, might actually have been upset if it were offered to him.

'You're having trouble?' Tiresias dabbed his mouth with a napkin. Light from candles and a single oil lamp fell across his face, smooth shaven and largely unlined, despite the mop of white hair. Without his glasses, his face was unfamiliar, the lie of bones and muscle oddly unspecific, the work of an artist who could not decide between man or woman. Tristram thought of the street hawker at Keleti station and dismissed the idea.

'I can get to sleep,' he admitted, huffing to cool another spoon of stew. Smelling caraway and chervil and pepper. 'But I'm having dreams.'

132

'Ah. Nightmares.'

'Bad dreams.' Tristram scooped up another spoonful, trying to appear unconcerned. 'I wake up. It's—' He blew on the stew but put down the spoon. He avoided looking directly at Tiresias, no matter the beggar was blind, and found himself meeting Rózsa's gaze. 'It's annoying,' Tristram mumbled.

'Well…' Tiresias scooped a little more stew. 'I'm sure we can find something that will help. Isn't that so, Rózsa?'

The housekeeper simply nodded.

'And, besides your sleep?' Triesias asked. 'How do you feel?'

His spoon paused before it reached Tristram's mouth. 'I'm quite sore still. And dizzy, sometimes.' He licked his lips. 'Better, of course, better than I was. Thanks to you. To you both. Of course. But…'

'The dizziness? The nausea?'

'Oh…' Tristram avoided looking at the blind beggar. 'Oh, they're still… They still bother me.'

'But less so.' Rózsa put down her spoon. 'You're much steadier than you were.'

'No.' He shook his head and, thinking that was something he should find hard to do, stopped almost at once. 'I am much better, though.' There was no place to look, not without appearing guilty. He sighed. 'I am much better. I should think—' Tristram pushed the bowl of stew away from him. 'I should think about finding somewhere to live, of leaving.'

'Why?'

'Because…'

'There's no need for you leave. Unless you want to.'

'I don't… I don't have anywhere to go.' The meal sat heavily in his stomach. 'Or money to go, come to that.'

'Then stay.'

Tristram managed to say thank you and, thinking that was too little, tried to say more but the words sounded hollow and tired. He bent over his meal, although the stew had grown cool and the lump in his throat made it hard to swallow. He excused himself, climbing to his room past the tailor's dummies along stairs lit only by whatever light found its way through the windows, unable to shake the notion that although Tiresias had mouthed the words, it had been Rózsa who had told him to stay.

'Perhaps you would like to walk?'

Tiresias paused, coat over his arm.

Tristram continued to stare out the window.

'I'm a little tired,' he managed.

'Still not sleeping well?'

'I'm fine, just tired today. Thank you, though. Perhaps tomorrow?'

Tiresias nodded and, moments later, the front door closed with a *snick*.

The chicken watched him from its usual spot on the corner of the kitchen table. Tristram ignored it.

Screaming woke him.

The house stood silent and darkness pressed close. Tristram gasped, unable to place the room, the light from the window as wrong as the shape of the window itself; rectangular, no longer a half-moon. Somewhere, there should be a bed and a figure under the blankets covering that bed. The floor creaked beneath him when it should have made no sound.

Tristram pressed a hand to his mouth, acid welling and bringing a cold flush that wound knots through his stomach.

The dream stood between him and the door; it glowered, demanding he keep quite and not draw anyone's attention. But there was no sound in the house but his own breathing and the thump of the pulse in his ears, the house undisturbed by his screams. Even the door was silent as he eased it open to peer into the hall, seeing a shape in the gloom and thinking it was one of the tailor's dummies before recognising Rózsa.

'Oh. Good evening.' He turned to go back into his room.

'Will you be able to go back to sleep?'

'I'm sure I shall.' It struck him that she must have heard his screams.

'I can make you something. It will make it easier to sleep.'

'No. I don't want to put you to trouble.'

There was dry scrape that became a whiff of sulphur and a flare of light. 'It's no trouble.' Rózsa lit an oil lamp, taken from the nook at the bottom of the stairs leading to the third floor, where her room was. She put the box of matches into the pocket of her dressing gown and led him downstairs. The chicken wandered out of one of the rooms across the hall from the kitchen. It watched him but made no sound.

'Really, please,' he tried again, 'it's nothing at all.'

'The tincture I made hasn't helped, has it?' She pumped water into the kettle as she spoke.

'I thought Tiresias made it.'

'Has it?'

He stood awkwardly, adrift in the middle of the kitchen. 'It's my fault.'

'You've not taken it?' Rózsa stopped spooning herbs into the tea pot.

'I've taken all of it.'

'Then—'

'I'd rather—' The image of a face staring through the rear window of a saloon car lodged itself in his imagination, refusing to fade. 'I'd rather not talk about it.'

Rózsa took a bottle down from a shelf, uncorking it and pouring a large measure, golden liquid tinting towards amber, into a wine glass. She held it out, gently swaying the glass to urge him to take it. 'Drink,' she told him.

He sniffed, finding honey and chamomile, dandelion and ginger amongst scents less obvious, second sip following the first, an alcohol glow spreading across his chest and throat.

'You were very badly beaten and you had the shock of having been assaulted by someone you thought to be a friend, to be dead, in fact.' She put another spoon of herbs in the pot. The kettle whistled. 'Not having nightmares would be strange.'

'Only dreams.' Tristram thought he had been too insistent, so he repeated the correction again, explaining his nights away as: 'Only dreams.' He drained the golden wine, the shock of alcohol after so long without imbibing leaving him a little giddy. 'It was a blow,' he admitted, watching steam shimmy from the spout of the teapot. Tristram nodded to himself. 'I went through this and worse during the War.' This seemed like explanation enough but scraps the of leaf waltzing around the brimming tea cup seemed not to believe him.

'She was beautiful?'

'Who?'

'The person you dream about.' Rózsa refilled his cup before putting the wine bottle back on the shelf. 'She haunts you.'

'No, no, not at all, not in the slightest, it's nothing of the sort, it's the shock, as you say,.'

'Sometimes you dream of her twice, even three times a night. I can hear, through the floor.' She pointed. 'My room is above yours.'

'Oh. Oh, I am sorry, I didn't mean to disturb you.' Tristram made to put down the cup. Rózsa pressed it back into his hands.

'I know.' She poured a little more tea into the cup and motioned for him to drink. 'Why do you say it's your fault?'

'I don't.' Tristram stared at her in confusion. 'It's not my fault. I didn't have any control over Voit, never did, you see, the man was—is, I should say—is quite headstrong.' He drained the tea.

'Tristram, I—'

'Thank you so much for the refreshments.' Tristram closed the kitchen door behind him before she could say very much more, taking the stairs two at a time.

Perhaps it was the wine, golden and heady, but he slept without dreaming, although a hundred different ways the conversation in the kitchen might have gone tripped over themselves as Tristram first lay down. He woke with a start, refreshed although the hour was still early. *Time to patrol—*

And he was out of bed before it came to him there was no need to be up and about, that the patrols and the caution had been futile. Tristram thought of the conversation with Rózsa and the need—no, no, the *desire*, it was his wish, Tristram told himself, it was his wish and *his* decision—not to see her that day, or ever, hurried him into his clothes and guided him with stealth and care down the stairs, to duck into the back corridor when the clunk of pots being taken from their hooks and wood being added to the range fire came from behind the kitchen door. Across the garden at a dash, only to worry the side door might be locked. But it was not even bolted. Tristram stepped out into the street and ran.

'She's only the housekeeper. Servants don't have opinions. Not if they know what's good for them.'

The rain had Vivien's voice.

He ran until he had to be sick, until the pain in his head was worse than the agony of being shot by the sniper. Tristram ran until another voice asked that he stop, a worse voice than Vivien's no matter how gently it spoke.

The rain spoke with its own voice again. It sounded no less accusing.

Tristram wandered for a time, careful not to stray too far in the direction of Szerb utca; to avoid Raven Passage, likewise. A whole city to wander in, turning back when the Danube came into view again, the clouds on the other side of the river soot grey and sluggish.

Finding Tiresias begging on the next street corner came as a relief.

'Ah, good, you decided to walk with me after all,' the beggar said when Tristram called out a greeting.

As they fell into step together, Tristram searched for something to say, some casual ruse to divert their path, from river and raven and old churchyard. But Tiresias set off northwards, speaking of the rain and the spring's slow arrival, that spinning into an anecdote, a tale, a myth, words escaping Tristram without him understanding them, content to *hm* and nod and forget to think, simply to walk.

When they returned to the tall house on the edge of the Jewish quarter, the prospect of seeing the blind beggar's housekeeper again no longer seemed daunting.

'What's this?' Tristram pointed to the design worked into the wrought iron grill set across the window beside the front door. 'I've not noticed this before.'

'No?' Tiresias guided a latch key into the lock.

'A cross and a Star of David?'

Tiresias traced the whorls of iron, finding and emphasising the loop rising from the T of the cross, enclosed within the overlapping triangles forming the six pointed star. 'An *ankh*. It's Egyptian, a symbol of life and soul.'

'Oh. I see.' Tristram did not. 'But the star…' A man in a long black overcoat and broad brimmed hat tilted against the rain hurried past, ringlets and beard, a nod of greeting to Tristram. 'Because we're…?'

'In this case, this represents Solomon's Seal. You see?' Fingers moving across the points where the triangles crossed. 'The microcosm in the macrocosm: *That which is above is like unto that which is below, and that below is like above.*'

'I don't understand.'

But Tiresias had turned the key and the door swung aside to present them with the white chicken, waiting patiently for their return.

It was still dark. Tristram glanced at the flight of stairs leading to the third floor before taking another step, stealthy so as not to disturb the dummies, or anyone else in the house.

Rózsa had made no comment when he returned with

Tiresias and, beyond asking after his health, made no reference to their talk of the night before. Tristram reassured himself this was how he wanted things to be.

It was still dark, early enough to ensure he was the only person in the kitchen. Working by touch and memory, Tristram found bread, cheese, gathering food enough for breakfast and lunch at least.

Fumbling, he knocked over a small pot, coins and notes tumbling across the table.

He had no money. The last of what he had been carrying had been spent the morning that Alba had—

Tristram swallowed.

The morning he had failed…

It did not matter, he reminded himself, scooping up coins, notes, all that mattered was that he had no money. Sára would not hesitate, Tristram thought, imagining her as he picked up the last of the coins and tucked them back into the pot alongside the rest.

Three mornings, three directions, none towards river nor raven nor old churchyard, the first even chosen to avoid the spot where he had met Tiresias the previous day. Each day, eventually, he and Tiresias met again.

'I wonder…'

Charcoal grey smeared half of the sky, clouds paler to the east.

'Yes?'

'It doesn't matter.'

And there was a smell of burning, of ash and cinder, there and gone amongst the scents of chimneys and motorcar exhausts. The drizzle did nothing to wipe it from the air.

'Please, Tristram, if there's something…?'

'I don't wish to pry.'

An aeroplane descended out the clouds above them, engine drone part of the breeze and the breath of the city as the machine turned eastwards, towards charcoal grey and the Danube and Buda beyond that. The buildings marshalling the street he and Tiresias ambled along to quickly hide the plane, block any view of the city across the river.

'There's no need.' Tiresias stopped walking. 'We've explained very little, Miss Farrenc and I, about—'

'Pardon? Who?'

'Miss Farrenc. Rózsa— Well, there you are.' The beggar spread both hands, a card player revealing every hidden card. 'You did not even know Rózsa's name. So ask, please. You must be curious, about me at least.' Tiresias smiled. Rain beaded each smoked lens and Tristram wanted to take the dark glasses and wipe them dry.

'Do you have—' Thinking of the peddler bringing wood, of Tiresias sitting in the niche outside the churchyard and, deciding it was a preposterous notion, veering to the next thing to come to mind. 'Your sight,' Tristram asked, 'you are partially blind?'

'Not in the slightest.'

'But you walk with such confidence.' Which sounded rude to Tristram, suggesting that he disbelieved Tiresias. 'You've been blind since birth?'

'An accident, I was not born this way. An accident or a blessing.' Tiresias smiled.

'I'm afraid I don't...'

'Oh, I was quite mortified when it happened, Tristram, but that was a long time ago and what I feel now and how I felt then... they're not the same.'

Tristram nodded. 'But still, such a big change, to be scarred—'

'Scarred?' Tiresias stopped walking. 'I don't feel scarred at all. This—' hand touching the spectacle frames, indicating the sightless eyes beneath— 'this has opened so many things for me.'

'I don't understand.'

'I was a person of position. A *man* of position.' Tiresias laughed although it was hard to see anything amusing in the claim. 'I gathered wealth almost as avidly as I gathered influence. It was very exciting at first, Tristram. And then, it stopped being exciting. No matter the gold I accrued, or the favours and the sway I could exercise over others, it left me dissatisfied. Nothing was enough.'

Tiresias began walking again. 'That was why I became obsessed with the locket.'

Tristram hurried to catch up.

'Some say it came from the East, from the forge of the greatest Taoist sage, or perhaps the closed temples of the High Himalayas. Others argue the locket was already ancient when the last Sage Kings of ancient India were washed from their palaces by the rising seas, when the Flood brought the great Atlantean age to an end, long before the first Emperor of China or the Pharaohs ruled over Egypt.'

They must be discussing different lockets.

'Not at all.'

Tristram froze.

'Is something wrong?' Tiresias turned back towards him.

'How did you— How could you know what I was thinking?'

'You spoke out loud.'

'I did?'

'Of course. A golden case which opens to reveal an image of Thrice Great Hermes between the presences of Sol and Luna? And on the front, a pelican, that symbol of eternal cycle and return? *Solve et Colagula*—the circling path of the *prima materia* risen into the eternal stone. There is only one locket, Tristram, as there is but one Mercurius, one Grail. Beyond doubt, we are discussing one and the same thing.'

'But Al—' He swallowed. 'But I was told the locket was an heirloom. And my landlord…' Tristram ran a hand through his hair, stubble growing out these past weeks. 'This makes no sense.'

'Please, be calm.'

'I'm going mad.'

'No.' Tiresias squeezed Tristram's arm. 'The locket has

many faces. All the same yet each its own—each different and yet, still, the same locket, just as the Mercurius is many and yet only and always simply the Mercurius.'

'That is—' *nonsense*— 'little comfort.'

Tristram pushed his hands deep into his coat pockets, fists clenched so tightly his arms began to shake.

The rain hissed.

In a little while, they began walking again.

'I also lost the locket,' Tiresias told him, 'and so lost my sight. Amongst other things. But I gained, as I say.'

'You never searched for it, once it was gone?'

'Of course.' They turned a corner, a wall coming up to the edge of the pavement beside them. 'But it was lost to me, not that I wanted to admit that. That was very difficult to do. For me, Tristram, the search was for something else. It had been all along but I could not admit that to myself, either. Sometimes, the hardest thing to know is our own motives and needs. In fact, they might always be the hardest to fathom.'

'What do you look for, then?' Tristram glanced up and stopped walking.

'Tristram?' Tiresias paused, head raising with a jerk. It was impossible not to think the blind beggar was looking at the spire and the onion dome on its top, or the niches along the wall where they had sat together in the past. 'I am sorry. I lost track of where we were. I would not have brought you here—'

Whatever else was said was lost in the *caw* and flutter of seven ravens rising into the grey sky from the gutters along Szerb utca.

The air tasted of smoke and parsley.

Tristram had slept long past dawn, kitchen deserted when he had finally come down. No sign of Tiresias or Rózsa, so he went out into the garden to sit amongst the beds of herbs and vegetables, as he had the night before, shivering against the damp air but putting off going back inside for as long as possible. There had been a glass of the golden wine waiting beside his bed when he had finally returned to his room.

The sky was grey, stained with a deepening charcoal towards the west.

Tristram took a breath, smelling parsley and rosemary, ready to assume the taste of smoke came from nearby chimneys, threads of vapour coiling from each to loose themselves among the clouds. He looked westward, wondering if the charcoal stain visible between the intervening rooftops might be smoke, a lot of smoke.

An engine droned closer.

'Would you like some tea?' Rózsa stood at the other end of the path.

Tristram had hardly spoken to her since the night his screaming had woken them both.

'Thank you,' he mumbled as she placed a steaming cup on the bench beside him. Yarrow, and fennel, and a waft of cinnamon. Almost enough to blot out the smoke. 'You don't have to wait on me, er, Miss Farrenc.'

She raised an eyebrow.

'It's not as if—' he fidgeted with the cup, turning it about in its saucer— 'I'm a paying guest.'

Stuffy— Vivien's voice loud in his mind.

'No, but you are a guest.' Rózsa turned to leave.

'I—' Tristram almost overturned the steaming cup in his haste. 'It's that I feel embarrassed. My dreams, the screaming, and I feel I'm imposing, I don't know how long I might stay or—or what I shall do when I leave.'

Silence. But, at least, she had not walked back into the house.

'I imposed. Once before…' Tristram faltered over the word 'once'. 'I imposed on someone's hospitality. I took advantage. Lied, in fact. I lied and…' There was no way of finishing this, none that he could see.

'You were desperate.' She watched him, sidelong, over her shoulder.

143

It might have been a question, so he answered, 'That seems a very poor excuse, wouldn't you say, Miss Farrenc?'

She turned away, saying simply, 'Call me Rózsa.'

The chicken did not step aside.

They exchanged a look.

Patiently, Tristram stepped around the bird and heaved the shopping bags on to the kitchen table. With a mad flapping of wings, the chicken followed, hopping from a chair to the table to peck at the contents of the string bags: cabbages, carrots, early onions and sacks of dried lentils and pearl barley and stoneground flour, not to mention several jars of paprika and Italian olive oil.

'Surely Tiresias can't be paying for all this from what he earns as a beggar?'

The chicken bobbed its head.

'Life isn't only about money.' Rózsa fed another wet sheet into the mangle, rollers squeaking as she turned the handle. Water trickled into a waiting tub.

'Tiresias might say that.' The kitchen smelt of fresh laundry and, subliminally, something acrid and burnt. Everything had smelled of smoke that morning, the western sky blotted with charred palls of dark ash. Tristram had considered going to the river to look across at Buda and thought better of it. He sniffed. The smell seemed stronger as he sat at the end of the table, near the door to the stairs, and he wondered if it came from inside the house after all. 'I don't think I agree with him, though,' he continued. 'One can't run this house on nothing, Rózsa.'

'True.' Rózsa took the sheet, pristine white, and offered it for the mangle to take again. 'The chicken.'

'What about it?'

Cogs locked and turned. 'Once every seven years, it lays a golden egg.'

'Oh, really…'

'It was a gift, from my master.'

Tristram stared at the chicken. The chicken stared back. 'From Tiresias, you mean?'

'Hm?' The crank paused and Rózsa looked up in confusion. 'No. My master, my teacher.'

'At school?' He found it hard to break stare with the bird. 'What a curious joke. But, anyway, if it's impolite of me to enquire about the house's finances, I apologise—'

'Do you—' Rózsa laid the freshly-pressed sheet across the clothes horse standing beside the range. The furnace door was slightly ajar, light escaping to touch the ice-white sheets with burnishes of flax and golden straw. 'Do you know what the lapis is?'

'A blue stone.'

'Not lapis lazuli. This stone is sometime known as the Elixir.'

She spoke as she worked on the laundry. Of base materials and phylosophickal gold. Of Mercurius, who was Hermes, but also an elixir found at the end of a long process but which was there right from the start. A stone that was no stone.

Tristram sat and listened, wanting to scoff but unwilling to cause offence. After a time, he lifted the chicken from the table and settled the bird on his lap, where it sat, clucking quietly to itself as Rózsa finished.

'You don't believe a word.'

Chickens laying golden eggs. Ankle chains of silver and gold. A blind beggar who could walk as easily without a cane as with, and seemed sometimes a woman, other times a man. 'I don't know what to believe.'

Rózsa placed a blue medicine bottle and a spoon on the table in front of him. 'Why?'

Careful not to dislodge the chicken, Tristram poured a dose of medicine. 'Because my life—' The tincture was fire on tongue and throat, a warmth spreading beneath ribs, a bloom beneath the skull. Tristram measured out a second spoonful, asking himself if he wanted to finish the sentence he had started. 'Because I doubt every single choice I have ever made and I doubt every single assumption I based those choices on. Isn't that terrible?'

Rózsa said nothing. But, in her silence, it was hard not to find his question turned back on him.

Scarlet darkness, vermilion stained and churning. A shape, half cloaked in shadow, shadows ruby threaded, carmine swirls that suggested a figure drawing itself into light reeking of iron and brimstone. Limbs fixed, unmovable. Needing to run. Needing to scream. Carmine and vermilion, scarlet hollows. Compelling. Run. Scream. Heart at the point of bursting and no breath, no escape, no escape, no—

He hit the wall. Spun, bedclothes become a straightjacket's embrace. Falling from the bed and then, only then, managing to scream. Scream strangled, too little. Vermilion and carmine, red stains on his hands and clotting the edges of vision, choking. Tristram dragged at another breath and screamed. Clawed at sheet and quilt and blanket. Beating against bed frame, against floor. Screaming away the redness and the shape within it. Shape wavering but not leaving.

Becoming.

Footsteps. A voice raised. Feet on stairs, coming up, descending. Voices asking questions. One voice just beyond the door.

Tristram screamed as the door opened and light flooded the room.

Honey yellow, welling into a flax verging on pure white, from there the light split, folding out of itself a green iridescence that drew up into a sapphire that dazzled but did not hurt, although, on its edges, it fluoresced into orange deeper than dawn, and that light became red.

Tristram shied back, wanting to scream again until he recognised the shape in the light, made out the hallway outside, the light pouring down the stairs from the floor above.

To snuff out. And leave the mundane light of an oil lamp, Rózsa setting it aside as she knelt beside him, Tiresias stumbling closer.

'I'm fine. I'm sorry. Just a dream.' It was hard to talk and catch his breath. Tristram let them help him up without further comment.

'Rózsa can get you something,' Tiresias volunteered.

'It must be late, I don't want to put you to any trouble.'

'No bother.'

She was not in dressing gown and night things but dressed in work clothes, a smock knotted about her waist, stained brown and yellow, a hole that might have been moths or acid. Tristram sniffed, smelling chemicals, acrid and sharp and, still confused from dream and waking, dismissing it all.

'I shall be fine in a moment.' He began to shiver. 'Please, I'd rather be alone.'

Rózsa paused in the doorway, Tiresias already halfway down the stairs to his room on the floor below.

No dreams, nor did the morning light shake him awake, although its grey face pressed close to the bedroom window, its features rain smeared. The corner of the room propped him upright—Tristram had not been able to go back to bed, the mattress too soft, too unlike the floor beneath the half-moon window. So he had sat in the corner, knees hugged to his chest, happy to be uncomfortable and cold. Unwilling to sleep for fear of dreaming.

There were voices in his dreams. And faces, sometimes painfully familiar, sometimes better forgotten—a junior boy at school he had laughed at when one of the older boys had torn down the youngster's trousers, laughed because Tristram had been relieved it had not been him, laughed to fit in with everyone else; or the sergeant he had had in his first command, a man of far greater experience who had looked at Tristram without hiding scepticism, *Do try not to kill us all, sir, that's all I can ask*, the sergeant dead within forty-eight hours when an artillery shell brought down a section of trench—but the scarlet and vermilion darkness scared him the most. He could not say why but better not to sleep than risk seeing it again.

Even so, sleep had eventually drawn him away from the corner and the chill of the room. No dreams except a shape, scuttling away before it properly registered. And, in the way of dreams, the shape turned into dreamlessness, and that gradually faded, took on form: scents, overlapping, one peppery—smoke, distant if acrid and itchy—the second metallic—a rough burr, caustic against his nose and the drift of sleep—and at last hooking and pulling him into wakefulness.

Frying onions, paprika and mushroom.

Warm, fragrant air enveloped Tristram as he opened the kitchen door, a welcome that made him grimace. Washing hung about the room, and dough was left to prove in a bowl beside the demijohns, wine pop, pop, popping as it fermented. Rózsa was tending a skillet on the range. The chicken sat on the corner of the table, Tiresias at its head.

Only the chicken and the housekeeper turned as Tristram closed the door behind him.

He cleared his throat. 'I'm sorry.'

It seemed ridiculous to be addressing the back of Tiresias's head. Tristram returned the chicken's unblinking gaze and glanced at Rózsa. He looked down at his feet.

'I am sorry for… It must be difficult, with me—dreams and—'

One hand sought out the other, fingers knotting. Aware of Tiresias turning, head bent to listen, Tristram thought he had said enough, that there was simply nothing more to admit.

'I'm sorry,' he said.

I am sorry. I do hope you forgive my fiancée, she can be a little headstrong…

I can only apologise for Vivien's brusqueness…

I am sorry…

148

I'm sorry, truly, I never intended to be gone so long, it was only ten minutes, only that and I didn't mean to leave—

'I didn't mean to fail...' Tristram saw a flash of white somewhere on the edge of vision, sure in that moment that it was not white but ash blonde, spun gold, like the links of a chain—*I'm sorry*—and he frowned.

'Why didn't you warn us?'

'Hm?' Tiresias looked confused. 'But I did.'

'You were guarding us. You and the peddler woman, bringing candles and sitting in that niche across the road, and yes, you warned me but you never said it was Voit, never warned me.' His voice was rising, quivering as his body quivered, one hand finding the other and gripping it tightly in a strangler's grip. 'I wished you'd left me there, you bloody fool, left me in the bloody snow, but you had to bring me here.' He could not cry, not in front of these people. Hand shielding his face, he turned away. 'Why?'

Tiresias began to speak, falling silent as Rózsa said gently, 'Because I thought we could help you. And because you had nowhere else to go.'

'I thought...' Tristram sniffed and straightened his shoulders. 'I've misunderstood—this isn't Tiresias's house, is it?'

'No,' she replied, 'it's mine.'

A tailor's dummy stood at the top of the stairs, a wooden arm extended in invitation.

Tristram hesitated. A bookcase blocked one doorway and a chest of drawers another. There was a second tailor's dummy, *papier mâché* eyes closed, its hand also raised towards the one and only door. Tristram hesitated.

There was something like relief when she did not answer his knock straight away. He turned to go.

The door opened.

There were fresh chemical stains on the smock, her hair escaping its bun, Rózsa's face flushed as she stood back, tugging stout gauntlets from her hands.

'Come in.'

'I'm disturbing you, I'll come back later.'

She stood back until he stepped into the room, unsure what he expected to find.

A lounge area, divided from the rest of the room by screens. Books, on shelves, in piles on the floor or draped over the arms of chairs. Soot stains on the Persian rug, the air scented with something sweet and resinous, and with smells more acrid. Steam began to hiss. Tristram turned to see Rózsa lift a kettle from a spirit stove and pour water into a tea pot.

'Sit.' She nodded towards one of the chairs. 'Just put the books on the floor. This tisane will be ready in a moment.'

Tristram glanced at one of the titles—*Novum Lumen Chemicum*—and put the stack of books carefully on the floor.

'Hops.' Rózsa proffered a steaming cup. Leaves danced across the surface. 'For calmness. Eat the leaves, they're good for you.'

'You're a herbalist.' He said it as if he had finally worked out the solution to a puzzle.

'That's one of my interests, yes.' She perched on the edge of another armchair, a cup cradled in her hands. Tristram was conscious of her studying him. He watched steam rise, hops gyre. Taking another sip, he searched for a way to begin and, remembering the many dinner parties he had endured, asked with inane brightness, 'Are you a scientist, like Madame Curie, then?'

'I wouldn't say that, Tristram, not exactly.' Rózsa sipped from her cup. 'You cannot feel guilt like this, it does no good.'

Tristram began to defend himself, arm jerking and slopping tea in the direction of the books piled beside the chair. Fumbling, he tugged a handkerchief from a pocket and dabbed at the spines—*Zwölf Schlüssel, Psychologische Typen, Parzival, The Wind Among the Reeds, Introitus*—stammering and apologising, trying to explain, 'If I hadn't lost the locket, I think if I hadn't—'

'You aren't the first to loose the locket.'

'Tiresias said something, that he—but it must be a different one.'

'No. It's the same one.'

'It can't be. Alba was very certain.'

Rózsa simply beckoned him to follow, behind the screens, a space given over to a bed, more shelves and bookcases and cabinets, ending at a spiral staircase leading up to the top floor.

Several of the walls had been knocked away to create a single room spanning the house. A laboratory: benches, retorts and distillation tubes; several boxes of earth beneath a row of windows, plants reaching from soil to light; books, of course, but also cases of insects, preserved and pinned and labelled, jars that (Tristram shied back a step) proved to have specimens in them, a heart the only thing he could identify with certainty. Gas flames licked the underside of glass flasks. Wheels spun to propel sparks from electrical contacts, the air tanged with ozone. At the far end of the laboratory, a ruddy glow filled the shadows.

'This is extraordinary.' Tristram turned another slow circle, gaze skimming past the red glow. 'Astounding. Are you an inventor? Like Mr Edison or Mr Tesla?'

'I'm... searching. Much as Tiresias searches but I follow a different path.' Rózsa topped up the liquid in a distillation column as she spoke. 'I do sometimes discover things along the way but that's not the reason for the search.'

Tristram leaned closer to a large, egg-shaped, glass flask, its sides speckled with condensation. Steam roiled within it. 'What is the reason, then?'

'To help things become more perfect.'

He frowned, shook his head.

'Some say this is about coming closer to the One.'

'*The One that was All... the Two that were One...*'

'Exactly.'

'I'm afraid I don't—'

'Alchemy.'

'Lead into gold?'

'Coming closer to the One. Think of it as a search for harmony. Or peace.'

'This is…' Tristram looked around the laboratory again.

'I think this is a path you are on yourself, Tristram.'

He shook his head, certain beyond doubt. 'I'm no mystic.'

'But your dreams, Tristram,' Rózsa told him softly, 'your dreams.'

She soaked fresh herbs, reserving the water and replacing it with fresh, macerating plants and roots already well-soaked as water nattered and trickled through pipes and flasks, circulating, plant matter packed into flasks and the flasks joined to pipes, water nattering, cycling around, a gas flame transforming it into steam, glass coils condensing, water rarified, running, to trickle, and soak through fresh herbs.

'It's very painstaking. And repetitious.'

Rózsa nodded. 'Repetition is important to the Work.'

Tristram was sure this should be boring, but he watched her go through stage after stage—maceration and washing and combining and distilling and steeping and macerating to wash and combine to distil, distillate going round and around the knotworks of pipe and column and tube and plants and roots steeped and simmered and—and he found himself comforted, mind not exactly wandering, not exactly floating, but in some way made loose, or free, or—

'I feel disloyal.'

The admission caught him by surprise. As Tristram tried to dismiss the words, Rózsa told him to go on.

'To…' He pretended the answer was hard come by, not obvious. 'To her memory.'

Rózsa glanced up. 'Not the young woman who was taken.'

'No. Vivien.'

'Yes.'

Neither spoke for some time. Tristram roused himself.

And told the story of the curé and the observation post, the curé's belief in an Adversary and an irredeemable, fallen world.

'Is that mandrake?' he asked, pointing to a root lying on the bench. Rózsa nodded. 'I thought alchemists worked with metals.'

'Alchemists work with a great many things.' Rózsa took a little of the mandrake and added it to a tincture. 'Let me show you.'

Heat rose and ebbed, coming from the furnace at the end of the laboratory in waves that seemed to draw breath, exhale, light flexing with each breathe, the fire behind the thick glass window in the fire box door whispering to itself, flames a voice just on the edge of hearing.

The fire paused as Rózsa waved Tristram closer. Watching.

He shook off the feeling and peered into the large, egg-shaped vessel held by the furnace's cupped hands. Condensation beaded the glass, the contents of the flask hidden inside clouds of steam: something dark, not exactly black but touched by the indigo of a midnight sky and the dank mould of a freshly dug grave. Wiping sweat from his forehead, Tristram moved closer.

Something flexed. Tristram flinched.

I should go, he had mumbled, wiping sweat from his face.

But she asked him to stay (*Stay...*), brewing tea from herbs and flowers picked from pots beside the skylights and the beds of rich hummus on the floor beneath, boxes filled with plants and mushrooms. Perhaps she had added mushroom to the drink because it had a dry, earthy taste to it as she asked him to stay and watch (*watch*), a taste that was hard to trace but which lingered, humming, as she asked him to watch over the furnace flames (*colour of straw into sunset, of blood orange, Tristram*), topping up his cup, adding a drop from a conical flask beneath a mass of glass tubes and columns, liquid condensing out of steam (*watch*), a soft, marigold-coloured liquid, a drop in his cup, taste lingering (*colour of sunset straw*) as she opened the firebox so he could see, furnace murmuring (*stay... watch*) as it painted trails across his vision, shapes hovering in the darkness whenever he looked away, a soft marigold (*straw into sunset*), a red (*of blood orange, Tristram*).

But, he had begun, but she explained she needed to go out and Tiresias was— well in any event, Tiresias was not in the house and she needed to go out, Rózsa had explained. Tristram drained his cup. Shapes turned and drifted with each blink: orange, yellow.

What happened to the light?

The skylights had closed their eyes, a darkness clotting the corners and the spaces beneath the benches. Orange shapes, yellow clouds, tumbling through slate grey and a deeper, darker shade that was part indigo, part the deep brown of fresh-turned earth, all of which parted (*now and then*) to give a glimpse of something red.

Tristram was staring into the flask.

What happened to the light? he had asked again.

Nothing, it's only that you're eyes are accustomed to the relative brightness of the fire.

And she had asked him to stay (*Stay*) and watch (*watch, Tristram*).

I...

A favour, not an obligation, Tristram.

It felt like an obligation. Because she had healed him. Because she had given him shelter. He had to give something in return, Tristram had thought.

The fire whispered.

And so he stayed.

Watching (*watch*).

The flames whispered. The flames moved, their fingers brushing against the window set into the firebox door.

Tristram saw pale oranges and yellows the colour of marigold. He saw flax, or the colour of an ash tree's heart. Ash blonde, the flames murmured, and he remembered how a shock of her hair would escape her headscarf, fall across her brow as she sat on the rug in front of the grate, a book open on her lap.

Shadows crept from under the benches to take the afterglow of the furnace fire, turn it back towards him as chestnut brown eyes and jet black hair, as skin pale and pure as marble, as— Tristram scolded himself. He was not here to daydream. The stool creaked beneath him as he sat forward. (*Concentrate...*)

The contents of the flask turned.

Mouth and throat dry. From the heat, he reminded himself, wondering if there was more tea. Head a little tight. From the heat. Condensation beading down the inside of the flask, drips sluggish, as sluggish as the contents of the flask.

Slate grey, shading into charcoal, into the brown of earth, fresh turned. And indigo. A night's sky on the other side of the glass, rain beading the flask, parting to give a glimpse of yellow, of orange, orange becoming rose, scarlet. Strands coiling, weaving a thread in ruby, a shadow in carmine.

Growing.

'Thank you,' Rózsa said again. This time, Tristram heard, blinking at the candles and oil lamps, the dozen or more bulbs glowing, the generator clattering loudly, unnoticed until Rózsa said, 'Thank you,' again.

'I brought supper.' She indicated a meal laid out on one of the benches—more tea and bread and steam rising from a bowl.

Tristram stared, surprised at seeing light and food laid out.

'Eat.' She helped him down off the stool.

There were slices of pepper in the stew, bright red

amongst yellow split peas. Rózsa broke bread and handed him a piece.

'Eat.'

Tristram's throat felt unused, as if he had not spoken in days. But that was the heat of the furnace, he explained to himself as he said thank you, took a gulp of water and thanked Rózsa again. The spoon rattled against the edge of the bowl, slices of pepper shaking as he brought them to his mouth.

'Should I watch tomorrow?'

'The Work is at an important stage. What do you think?'

Tristram scooped another spoon of stew.

'I don't know.'

'But you know what to look for, don't you, Tristram?'

Steam, rising from the spout of the tea pot and from the cup beside him.

'Yes.'

Steam from the bowl of the spoon, the spoon filled with yellow split peas.

'That's settled then.'

Yellow peas and red. Red pepper.

'Yes.'

Red pierced—

He was dreaming.

Red pierced the darkness—

It felt like a dream.

Red pierced the darkness sweating out of the flask. In shades of brown, deep and rancid; in skeins of indigo, deep enough to recall the night, the darkness oozed and swelled, gathering around him. A twilight, a pit, deeper than the sun could ever reach, dank and empty, empty inside. Better to ignore it, deny the emptiness, although there were reminders everywhere: at a picnic, held under a sun of splintered jet, a parasol tilted to keep off its rays and robbing her face of detail and form; and in snow, falling, walls blocking the wind so the flakes bobbed, turned black as the emptiness seeped into each one, black flakes settling across

156

the pages of a book, settling into drifts around the foot of the stone bench and slowly, oozing and creeping, swallowing the gravestones nearby, the emptiness erasing her from the bench, leaving only a space in the air, darker than any other spot in the graveyard, a space that went on reminding him of someone sitting on the bench, reading from a book.

It had to be a dream, the red coming from the flask as surely as did the emptiness and the dark.

Red pierced the darkness, wrenching it aside, tail flex shattering the flask, sinuous body arching, wings unfurling around him. Scales glimmered: vermilion, scarlet, eyes carved of wet ruby staring, coming closer, staring at him.

He tried to look away but this was a dream and wherever he looked it waited for him.

Coils growing tight, shimmering, vermilion and scarlet, as they began to shrink, wings becoming arms and serpent's face moulding itself into a woman's features, pale and wrinkled with age: an elderly woman dressed in vermilion and scarlet. She leaned closer to him and he could smell her, feel the cool damp of her skin as she pressed a hand across his mouth—

'I need to go out again.'

Tristram startled, stool rocking beneath him.

'I need to go out again,' Rózsa told him. 'Can you watch a little longer?'

'Watch?' He sipped the tea, expecting it to be at least warm, certain Rózsa had left only a few moments earlier. But the tea was long cold, although its taste was the same, lingering on after he drained the cup.

'I fell asleep,' he admitted. 'I'm not sure I can do this.'

'Can you try?' Rózsa asked.

No matter where he looked, the furnace light curled and twisted, colour of sunset, colour of blood orange behind his eyes when he blinked. He wanted to leave, seemed to remember saying that he was about to go, shifting so the stool muttered beneath him.

Tristram licked his lips, mouth dry beneath the taste of the tea. In the next moment, he promised, he would get up and leave, his muscles tensing, the stool shifting, muttering until he became still with the promise that in the next moment, or the one after that, he would leave.

The furnace brushed a hand across his face, hand the colour of straw into sunset, of blood orange, its taste fixed on his tongue.

The contents of the flask turned, dew beading the inside of the glass, droplets slipping, each meander pulling at his thoughts, the stool silent, no longer muttering because he no longer moved.

Only waited.

She wore vermilion and scarlet; not scales but cloth; not wings and tail but robes billowing in the last of the furnace's heat.

Tristram stared as the flask opened, an oyster shell parting its lips for her to climb from its mouth, straw into the colours of sunset, blood orange ripened into vermilion and scarlet, heat of fire become the colour of scales and that colour the colour of her robes, of her lips vivid against otherwise pale skin.

The furnace ticked, already cold. She took another step closer and Tristram managed to look away, hands beating the air, trying to ward her off as she came closer. Shadows sweated from the robes, leaving nowhere to hide, nowhere to look but into her face. Tristram saw wrinkles, saw sagging flesh and the horror of Time's passing. And he remembered:

I shall never grow old.

You'll stop time? he had replied.

Don't believe me?

I would believe anything of you, Vivien.

Did you?

The woman took hold of his wrists, grip tightening as he tried to pull free.

Did you?

Her mouth did not move, yet there was the question; in every place he looked, beneath every word he could manage to think, among the wrinkles, in skin pale and fragile, so lifeless compared to vivid scarlet, to vermilion in the shadows.

Did you believe anything of her?

Her mouth did not move, yet the question was there.

'I betrayed her.'

How?

'By...' Tristram squeezed his eyes tight shut but she looked at him out of the darkness, her eyes black, widow's black because the furnace was dead and cold, black because there was nothing in them, only emptiness. Only contempt, Tristram thought, catching sight of himself reflected in the empty black. 'By not, by failing to do— By failing,' he managed, his mouth not moving although the excuses were there.

Vivien? Or Alba?

'Failed.' He looked into her eyes. Whether his own eyes were open or not, there was no choice but to look into her eyes. 'Failed.' The word came again. 'Failed at...'

She forgave you. You know that. When Mátyás—

'No.' He shook his head. 'Not Vivien, she would never—'

When Mátyás—

'Never.'

He wondered if she could see herself in his eyes as he saw himself in hers, his face growing larger as the woman in vermilion and scarlet drew closer. Until he could taste her breath in his own; until their lips touched.

Gasping, choking, Tristram jerked away, punching wildly, striking out and hitting—

Empty air. Only empty air.

He tumbled off the stool, floor catching him before he could fall any further.

Afternoon light scurried between the benches, hiding

159

behind the scaffolds of glassware. In the distance, an engine droned, a bell insistent, another joining in the clatter.

Tristram sat up, raking the back of his hand across his lips. Only the taste of the tea lingered in his mouth, nothing else. He had been dreaming. It had felt like a dream.

Unruffled, the fire muttered and cracked its knuckles.

Fierce heat poured out as he yanked open the furnace door and squinted at the flames. Seeing yellows tending to orange, relieved the fire was still strong, still burned at the right temperature. Yellows tending to orange, oranges merging into vermilion, vermilion into scarlet—

There was movement behind him.

Wanting to pretend it was not there, Tristram began to turn away, expecting robes and pale, wrinkled skin. But the movement came again and there was no stopping his glance towards it. Seeing one of the skylights open, a sparrow perched on the window frame.

The bird began to sing, notes a hand beckoning, pointing.

'You must follow.'

Rózsa stood beside him.

'But the furnace—'

A bloom of colours was shot through the flask, blackness almost completely faded.

'The fire was just right.' Rózsa gently pushed him away from the furnace. 'This stage is complete. You should go.'

Birdsong called again. 'I don't understand.'

'She left the vessel. You kissed.'

'No. No, we didn't.' The sparrow flexed its wings, ready to take flight. 'I couldn't—'

'You can't stop.'

'I don't—'

'Go.' Rózsa pushed him. 'You have to follow, Tristram.'

The sparrow leapt into the air.

Tristram dived forward, horrified the bird was diving out the window. But it bobbed and winged across the laboratory to disappear down the spiral staircase. Tristram's feet set the funnels and glass columns rattling, the stairs drumming. Slithering down the last few steps he saw the sparrow swooping between the folding screens, out into the hallway, tailor's dummies pointing out the way it had gone as he chased down each flight of stairs. Into the kitchen, the sparrow swerving around the half-open door, into the entrance hall where the sound of the front door opening became Tiresias's voice, rising in surprise, sparrow twitting out a warning. Tiresias falling against the door, leaving Tristram no choice but to vault over the blind beggar. Leaping after the bird, leaping over the threshold.

And finding himself not running but walking across open meadow. Recognising, in the next step, the fields outside the town of Arberth.

Blankets and hampers. His father holding forth: '*Arbeth* being, in Lady Guest's *Mabinogion*, you see...' Vivien's father searching loudly for mustard, his glass held out in expectation of a refill of claret. And Tristram's mother pretending to follow some long, involved tale of horses and hunting and a church bazaar Vivien's mother was recounting. Family friends sat close, feigning interest or trying to monopolise attention. A cork popped. Cutlery clinked against good china. Sunshine. April warm enough to bring blossom to the gorse bushes.

He remembered this picnic. The spring of 1914, a memory faded with the years that had passed and as immediate as if he had been distracted a moment, lost in reverie and brought back to polite expressions and asinine conversation, the scud of cloud across the pallid sun, back to this place where Pwyll, Prince of Dyfed, was said to have had his throne.

Vivien's laugh rose and fell on crow's wings.

She sat at the very edge of the party, parasol angled to protect her complexion from the ravages of the sun. A plate lay beside her, food untouched. Her wine glass empty, once again.

'More wine, m'dear?' Aubrey bounded to his feet, snatching up the glass.

'Oh, let someone else fetch it, Aubrey.'

'Only too happy, Vivien.'

Despite the parasol, the sunlight could not leave her be. It made her golden, perfect and beyond comparison.

'You're a lucky fellow, Tristram.' Vivien's father appeared beside him, claret cup in one hand, other brushing ineffectually at crumbs and grease stains, working them deeper into his waistcoat. 'Quite the beauty, Vivien. Quiet the, erm—' Her father gestured with the glass, wine slopping. 'You'll know, I'm sure—goddess in the shell, hm?'

'Venus,' Tristram murmured, watching Vivien flirt with Aubrey. Strange he had not noticed it before since she was quite blatant about it.

'Really?' Her father looked perplexed. 'Could have sworn it was— Oh well, no matter. Like a goddess, though, what?'

The sun pressed closer, whispering, flames bringing a sweat that beaded and ran, forehead to temple. 'Yes,' Tristram managed, mouth dry. Strange he had not noticed this before, the flirting, the flagrance of her behaviour. The contempt. 'Very fortunate.' Flames whispered. His stomach clenched. 'Most fortunate to have Vivien as my fiancée, sir. Do please excuse me,' Tristram said, not waiting for her father to reply, ignoring Aubrey, asking Vivien to go for a stroll.

'I don't feel like walking, Tristram.'

Persuading.

'It will help your lunch settle, Vivien.'

Insisting.

'I was having a perfectly charming time without walking around this hillock.'

The Dragon's Seat, where Pwyll sat each autumn. Where he had a vision of Rhiannon on a roan horse that had red ears.

'You must stop.' Tristram kept his voice level. 'It can't go on.'

'Darling Aubrey, you mean?' Vivien pretended to be bored.

'Stop it.'

'Oh, but Tristram, dearest,' Vivien laughed, 'I can't. You enjoy being humiliated far too much for me to stop.'

'What a wretched thing to say.' The ground pressed beneath his feet, clouds hunching, summoning a crow to circle and watch as he stammered, 'I won't tolerate this any longer, Vivien.' Air oppressive, flames whispering. 'I simply won't—'

Vivien pressed her face close to his. 'Would you like to watch?' Her breath against his skin. 'Wouldn't it be wicked and wonderful? To watch me and Aubrey?'

He wanted to push her away and run. Soil and rock shifting beneath him, crow giving voice to the weight of the day, each grass blade and petal on the gorse bushes straining, writhing.

'We never had this conversation, did we?' he managed. 'I told myself I was imagining you and...'

Vivien sighed. 'No, this didn't happen.' Her voice was the crow's. Or the wind, soughing through grass and branch. Her voice was a shadow passing across the field of Gorsedd Arberth. 'It didn't happen but you imagined it had. Over and again.' And she turned away, shadows drawing the hem of their dress across dense clover and sedge. Sun cupping his skull.

Tristram staggered, faced flushed. He tried to think of something, a denial or an excuse.

He looked up.

The horse whinnied, stepping from behind the earth mound where Pwyll, Prince of Dyfed was said to have had his throne.

She wore vermilion and scarlet, wind hiding her face behind her long, grey hair. He could imagine her expression. It would be stern and unforgiving. She would be whispering.

So Tristram ran.

A lamp post seized his shoulder and jerked him back on to the pavement before he could run into the road. A lorry, several cars close behind: traffic ground up and down Andrássy út. Tristram held his breath, waiting. But the boulevard did not turn into grass meadow and the mound of earth where a prince once set his throne, any more than the acrid breeze turned warm, nor the dull clouds part to reveal April sunshine. Tristram held his breath, listening. But the city of Pest droned and rattled, its pulse drowning out most other sounds. Tristram was about to give up when, faintly, faintly, a scrap of melody bobbed on the sour breeze.

The song of a sparrow.

He followed. Turning back; circling to go forward. Breaking into a run. Across the next crossroads. Hearing fire bells, clamour louder as the birdsong beckoned him towards the river, streets growing packed, crowds milling as some tried to push deeper into Pest, others wanting to get closer to the hammering bells and the steam whistles blaring along the shore. He caught another snatch of song amidst the tumult, song pulling him on until, at last, the Danube heaved itself up to glower at the cars shying across the pavements to let through the fire engines haring towards Széchenyi bridge.

Smoke tumbled over the hills of Buda, blotting out rooftops and towers, flames darting between the clouds, yellow of straw tending to sunset, blood orange deepening into rose. Countless fires walked the hillsides, rowdy and hungry, pretending to ignore the Danube only to creep closer when the river was distracted by the steam launches and boats thronging its surface. Embers swooped to perch among the rails and stanchions of the bridge, winking out with the promise that soon one of them might take hold, carry the fires across into Pest, the smoke already bringing an early darkness to both cities.

Through this chaos, the sparrow's song was faint, almost but not quite lost.

Tristram shrank away, watching the river churn, its expression stern and brim with contempt. He could not cross the Danube and the river mocked his cowardice. Easier to follow the throngs stumbling off the bridge. Soot-stained and eyes wide, lugging suitcases or bundles, soothing crying children or simply running, haste and hurry driving the tide into Pest, a river as turbulent as the Danube. Easier to be taken by this current, so much easier to be pushed and harried further away and further away from bridge and fire and Buda under deepening cloud.

No sparrow song. Only crowd and tumult and the Danube's contempt.

A few steps carried by the current. A step against. A few more, turning into pushing and struggling to squeeze his way back to the bridge, focus on the road underfoot or the nearest gap in the crowds, not asking what made him strive for Buda any more than he let himself look at the river.

It was a little easier on the road than trying to fight through the pedestrian walkways along the parapets of the bridge. Dodging between straggles of cars and vans and horse carts, ignoring irate drivers whenever the press of people moving between the vehicles in the opposite direction forced him on to a car's bonnet, a van's roof. Anything to keep moving against the tide.

Fire bells clanged, engines and voices yelling back. Tristram paused, straining, sure he had caught a hint of birdsong. Close, to be heard against this uproar. He clambered up on the back of a cart, carter and his family ignoring him as he stood and listened.

Engine drone corkscrewed out of the twilight, gathering itself to burst through the smoke clouds, aeroplane banking sharply to swoop low over the bridge.

Tristram lost his balance as he ducked, falling to the road.

'You can't be a knight on a quest, Tristram.'

Vivien leaned over him. She wore white, gown spotless no matter how the smoke wafted and spat.

'It's not in you.'

When he turned away, Vivien clamped hold of his chin and forced him to look her in the eye.

165

'It's not in you, Tristram.'

A great and terrible goddess, Vivien was beautiful, a flawless beauty cold as the air, as the grey wind, as the shingle beneath. No longer aware of road or bridge, only pebbles, hard and unyielding; only Vivien, no less hard and unyielding.

'It's not you,' she whispered as she tried to kiss him.

Tristram jerked out of her grasp, mumbling apologies a moment later, wanting more than anything to have her forgiveness. The surf turned scornful, the beach heaving and the buildings of Aberystwyth turning away from him.

'Always so *proper*,' Vivien spat.

'I wanted to love you,' Tristram pleaded. 'I would have tried—'

'But it never was love, Tristram.'

Vivien turned away from him, flinging her arms around a man passing by, only to push him aside and snatch a woman into a passionate kiss. The woman faded on the blustering wind, no more solid than smoke.

'Just responsibility,' Vivien told him, wiping her hand across her mouth. 'You told me so yourself.'

'But we could have learned, couldn't we?' Shingle and sand rose and fell, sometimes soot grey, sometimes cast with a deep indigo.

'Is that what you thought?' Vivien turned to kiss another man and Tristram scrambled to his feet, jealousy's puppet. But, when he spun the man to face him, it was not Aubrey. It might have been anyone.

'You don't love yourself, Tristram.' Her voice was gulls and surf, the clamour of bell and flame.

'No, that's not—'

Seeing a glimpse of vermilion, vermilion and scarlet, her face half-veiled by gathering darkness.

Tristram could not look.

She rested a hand on his shoulder, not demanding his attention, not asking for anything. He found he was studying her face, each line and imperfection, expecting to find rebuke, or to see himself mirrored in her eyes.

Sparrow song trace itself through the crash of surf, surf becoming engine and alarm bell, the thud of feet and rasp of breath, licks of flames rising above the hills, raucous and wild, and still, faint though it was, Tristram heard a snatch of song.

He pushed the last few steps through the crowds until, at last, he set foot in Buda.

A roof bloomed into a million sparks, flames striking out in rage.

Tristram reared away, fires barring another way up the hillside.

There had been no hint of the sparrow for a while, the last snatch of its song lost amongst the streets above him. No choice but to keep climbing, the blaze forcing him to retreat and circle, circle and climb, to retreat again, oblivious to falling cinders and debris.

Always, it seemed, the fires waited for him.

He found the alleyway by accident, grouping through the gloom, feeling the cobbles rise and the slope grow steeper before he guessed what this might mean. The insect rustle of cooling wood and masonry grew louder as he climbed, fires retreating, finished with this place and leaving only an unsettled glow to stain the cloud cap overhead.

The hill rose beneath him.

The voices were hushed, lost for a time in the rasp of his breathing as he scrambled across heaps of brick, collapsed walls still hot to the touch.

'Hey, buddy, watch where ya—'

Someone grabbed hold of him, pinning his arms before he could react to the pale smudge of a face beneath the broad brim of a fedora.

'Jesus, it's—'

Tristram tried to pull away but an elbow jabbed into his ribs, an arm tight across his windpipe.

'Hey, Red, it's the fella from the station.'

Another shape appeared, face nothing but a haze of

167

shadow as it pushed close.

'So it is.' Red took an automatic pistol from his coat pocket. 'Guess the shoe's on the other foot, pal,' he hissed.

'I deliberately missed you,' Tristram managed.

'Yeah, yeah, I know.' Red shrugged. 'That's why there's no hard feelings. But I got a job to do, see? So—' the automatic pointed into the night— 'you comin' easy?'

No need to ask where.

IV
RUBEDO

THE HOUSE STOOD in a wasteland of clinker and soot. No lights showed inside and the glow of the fires clinging to the base of the hill pointed to missing windows, walls pitted and streaked with smoke; suggesting the house must be abandoned like the few others still standing nearby. Each breath tasted of char, the air oily to the touch. Yet Red walked between heaps of rubble towards the rear of the building, the other gangster prodding Tristram to follow. Tristram glanced back before the house blocked all view, glimpsing more rubble in the near distance, hilltop razed except for the broken tooth of a bell tower above the shell of a church.

A low whistle. A face emerging out of shadow in response, guard standing back to let then into the house.

Curtains hissed. The scrape of a match, brimstone crackle bringing a lamp to life.

Tristram squinted against the dazzle, Red already knocking at a connecting door. He waved Tristram through.

Nox was immaculately groomed, as always. He sat in a space cleared of debris and ash, enamelled picnic boxes, a plate and silver cutlery laid out on a folding table beside him. A tall man was pouring white wine into a crystal glass. He jerked his head towards a chair.

'Park it.'

'Floyd, he is our guest.' Nox piled caviar on a bliny. 'Do sit, Tristram, do'

'Guest?' Tristram sat slowly.

Nox sipped wine and shrugged. 'Very well, prisoner, if you prefer.' He wiped his mouth on a linen napkin. 'You have work, I believe, Floyd.'

Floyd pushed back the folds of overcoat and suit jacket beneath, hands on hips and the butt of his automatic pistol on display.

'I'll leave Red, boss.'

'Both go,' Nox snapped.

Floyd straightened, mumbling an apology as he scuttled from the room.

Nox drank more white, napkin spotless even once he had

dabbed his lips again.

'I am not an angry or vindictive person, Tristram,' he began, pausing to spread pâté across a sliver of toast. 'I will admit that fiasco at the station was somewhat embarrassing.' A smile congealed on his face. 'I dislike such obstacles. They are always unnecessary.' Nox drained his glass, sloshing more from the bottle. He laughed. 'But I am not a vindictive person, Tristram—may I call you Tristram? Of course I may, I know you so well. Did you know that? No, please—' Nox waved away words Tristram had not spoken— 'please, there is no need for coyness: that bank of yours, the time in the house of that troublesome little man who effects those ridiculous spats. I knew where you and my... where Alba were hiding. I had you under surveillance all along. You seem shocked, Tristram.'

Tristram did not move.

'I am less interested in you than in your relative, Voit.'

'We're not related.'

'Indeed?' Nox shrugged. 'I have information to the contrary, but as you wish.' He took another drink.

'Voit is not—'

'Enough—' The glass slammed on the table, wine spattering. 'As I say,' Nox continued in a calmer tone, 'it is of no consequence.' He dabbed wine from his hand. 'I imagine she told you about her childhood, about the locket? Yes?'

'Alba? Yes, she spoke—'

'No doubt, no doubt. It will have been lies, Tristram.' Nox refilled his glass. 'My— Alba bends the facts to suit herself.' Glass cradled to his chest, Nox leaned back and began: 'Only I know the truth...'

I can confirm that I am of noble birth.

When my parents died, I was adopted by Alba's father. My mother was a distant relative of his late wife, you see. He was reluctant to give me a place at first. I came to think he wanted no part of me because my family was quite poor, despite our lineage. Indeed, my entire inheritance was

172

contained in a small wooden box, secured against the day of my twelfth birthday. In time, I learned that my poverty made no different to the old man.

In any event, he did take me in.

(Nox paused to drain his glass.)

My adoptive father's estates were deep in the forest and it seemed to me that I entered an enchanted place, an impression bolstered by my first sight of Alba—luminous and beautiful even at so very young an age. I thought I had found my way into a fairy tale. Alas, my new father was anything but charming, a cold man, crippled by an accident and by the death of Alba's mother. I suppose that is still something from a fairy tale, don't you think?

In any event, it was later that very first day that I met Voit. And Voit's younger brother.

(Nox stared at Tristram, who remained silent.)

Voit was related to my adoptive father, much as I had kinship to his late wife. Father—if I may use the term—had taken the brothers away from their parents, whom Father believed were incapable of looking after the boys. Voit lost no time in bragging to me that he would be inheriting Father's estates and that I would remain a pauper. I said nothing, not then, but I soon learned there was no reason to hold my tongue with Voit; nothing could ameliorate his capacity for spite and cruelty. The way he treated his brother... The boy was like a dog to him— You do remind me of that boy, Tristram. Faintly, it is true, and yet—

In any event, it was a matter of weeks before the boy left the household. Alba told me he had been sent to a sanatorium. Voit, the braggart, insisted the boy had gone to live with wealthy relatives abroad—not as wealthy as *he* would be one day, naturally, but wealthier than I could ever hope to be...

I did not set out to compete with Voit for our father's affections. It was inevitable, even so, that Father should come to favour me. Voit was a detestable sycophant and, in time, Father saw that I was the most worthy of his children. Voit, I hardly need add, utterly refused to acknowledge publicly this shift in our relationships. Rather, he did all he could to undermine my confidence in the new state of affairs, an underhand and clandestine campaign but I saw it in glances, in the tone of his voice and the smallest of gestures. I saw it, Tristram.

And so came my twelfth birthday and the opening of the wooden box. Yes, it contained the locket, as I'm sure you suspected. A note, in my mother's hand, explained the locket had been in her family for generations. It had been the source of our wealth, until my real father had contrived to squander our legacies and fortunes.

Voit was consumed. He wanted the locket, even claiming it was his, stolen from his family by mine, its loss the cause of his parents' death, which we had had news of only the week before—tragic, of course, but hardly my fault. In any event, the appearance of the locket caused my adoptive father distress, something which concerned me more than Voit's blustering.

My adoptive father revealed that the locket was a gift, you see, from him to his first and greatest love—my mother. I was astounded, Tristram, although it made me feel closer to the old man; but for some twist of fate, he might have been my father. He told me the locket was ancient, older than I could imagine. To be its guardian was to be marked as the true heir of the estates and the family's wealth. But that luck had been perverted by my true father, who had beguiled my mother, tempting her away from my adopted father and bringing bad luck to everyone.

My adopted father put the locket away for safe keeping and I knew then that he intended I should inherit everything.

(*Nox paused, hesitating over the tin boxes of delicacies.*)

Alba was sent away to school.

(*He cut himself a wedge of cheese.*)

Not that I played with her or indulged in her company— I was preoccupied with studies, with Voit's bating, with my adoptive father—but I felt a loss at her leaving. Even Voit seemed to notice it and he became less aggressive, more withdrawn. The friction between us lessened and I was willing to allow him to be friends with me.

Well…

Nox stared into his wine.

Tristram cleared his throat. 'He didn't want to be friends?'

'Hmm?' Nox drained his glass, choose something else to eat. Tristram ignored the rumbling of his own stomach.

'No.' Nox sat back. 'It was a ruse. A year-long pretence so that no one would be suspicious when, at the end of that year, Voit tried to steal the locket from our adoptive father's study. We fought, he and I, Voit screaming loudly that the locket was his and that Father had taken it from me for this reason alone.

'I broke his arm.' Nox laughed at the memory. 'And we were each dispatched to boarding school. A punishment in Voit's case. In mine, all the better to prepare me for taking over the family's affairs.'

There was the sound of movement in the corridor outside, although no one came in.

Nox waved a hand. 'I underestimated him.'

Voit was named heir.

'I confronted Father, abandoning my studies to return to the estate the moment I heard. He was distressed, insisting he had been compelled—'a legal necessity' was how he put it: it was a 'legal necessity' that a blood relative be named heir. Voit had engineered it. It was not my father's doing.'

Nox studied his reflection in the facets of the wine glass.

'It was not my father's choice,' he murmured, before dismissing the thought. 'Voit was industrious—not only had he inveigled the locket out of Father's possession, he had got himself engaged to Alba.'

Nox travelled to Prague where Voit was studying, the confrontation quickly becoming physical. 'Voit struck me—a broken bottle.' Nox shifted, free hand touching the top of his leg.

The fight grew more desperate, continuing even as an overturned lamp strewed flames around the room. 'When the flames caught, Voit made his mistake, leaving me to burn. The whole lodging house burned down but I was rescued and my injury gave irrefutable weight to my accusations. I made a full report to the police, and I spoke to Voit's masters and peers. No one harboured anything but enmity for him when I finished, his reputation utterly destroyed. Justice served, you see, because the locket was lost in the conflagration.'

With Voit still at large, Nox returned to the family estates as soon as possible. Although there was no sign of his adopted brother, news of the fire had reached home before him.

'I thought my father would be worried on my behalf but...' Nox peered at the wine bottle until he convinced himself it was empty. 'Voit's poison, Tristram, it spreads, it corrupts. My father was overwrought about Voit's disappearance and the loss of the locket. I tried to explain, that Voit was an upstart, that Voit had started the fire deliberately, that his stabbing me had been an attempt on my life and nothing less. But Father... had been corrupted. The scale of Voit's plot against me was much, much greater than I had suspected.'

His adopted father disowned Nox for attacking Voit and causing him to disappear.

Nox had doctors examine his adopted father and declare him insane.

'What choice had I? Understand, Tristram, I loved him but he had been warped by Voit's poison and the love he had shown me was gone and forgotten. But I remembered his plans for me, I knew what it was that Father truly wanted for me.'

And so Voit took control of the entire estate. Suspecting the Voit might have spies amongst the staff, he had them all sacked and thrown off the family's lands. The house—already more castle than mansion—was fortified, the boundaries of the estates guarded day and night while Nox employed agents to hunt down Voit.

'And I had Alba brought back. It was unsafe for her to be away from the house. I tried to impress this on her.' Nox frowned. 'She seemed not to believe the degree of threat and wanted to return to school. Obviously, I could not allow that and I had no choice but to confine her to the house. For her own good and... yes, I admit, I wanted her close for other reasons.'

He declared his love for her.

'At first she claimed that she thought of me as a brother, as family.' Nox dismissed this notion. 'I could hear it in her voice, the lies. I told her I would not tolerate deceit. Alba pretended it was the severity of my wound that concerned her, that I should place my recovery as my priority. And when I made it clear that I was not to be trifled with in this manner, she made up some nonsense about not respecting me for what I had done to our father. Of course, since that was for his own good, there was nothing to her excuses.

'I knew, without doubt, that Voit had already poisoned her.'

Nox placed a lid on one of the tin picnic boxes, wiping his hands on a napkin. 'I would have sent her away, Tristram, given her a degree of latitude in the organisation of her life. But I... needed Alba. I could do nothing to stem my affection for her and I could not bear for her to be far away from me for long, not with Voit's whereabouts uncertain, not...'

He stood, adjusting the drape of his overcoat.

'And my lawyers assured me that, with her co-operation, there was no avenue for Voit to challenge my rightful claim over the family's interests. I did not doubt I was doing what our father had wanted and what was just. An empire is much easier to defend than a castle, or a house in the middle of a forest.'

Nox had the house pulled down. With so many holdings and interests, it was easy for him to become nomadic, resident nowhere for very long. As his agents could find no sign of Voit, it seemed likely his adopted brother might have died in the fire after all. But Nox refused to relax, sure that Voit would return.

There was a knock. Floyd appeared around the door and nodded.

Nox dabbed his mouth with the napkin before dropping it on the floor.

'I was not wrong, Tristram.'

They darted through the clinker and soot, shadows amongst shadow. The small brigade of Nox's irregulars fanned across the waste, drawing a noose tighter around the gutted church, the derelict wavering in the glow from the fires surrounding the hilltop but otherwise still and lifeless. Yet Floyd's patrols had reported seeing Voit inside, and Voit had not been alone.

Red materialised out of the gloom and dragged Tristram into shelter behind a pile of rubble. 'Wait,' the gangster hissed.

Ahead, a few silhouettes stopped advancing, settling into shadow themselves. Waiting. And still no reaction from within the church: *Perhaps Floyd's guards had seen what they wanted to see—* Tristram dismissed the thought as soon as it came, swallowing hard, the sharp copper taste remaining on his tongue and his stomach clenching tighter; despite a clammy sweat making him shiver, his hands remained steady. He wondered if there would be whistles to signal the start of the assault.

No whistles.

A thrum built through chest and ears, ground beginning to tremble as the vibration knitted itself into the beat of engines, a vast shape barging through the clouds to hang over the hilltop, dirigible watchful and threatening and joined, moments later, by a flock of aeroplanes, swooping and turning, manic swifts chasing invisible insects and finding, instead, flares leaping in answer to their circling, coals arcing from Nox's front line, fusillades of rifle and pistol shots opening up, underscored by the steady hammer of sub-machine guns, muzzle flashes bobbing as the front line moved in on the ruined church.

'Nox is going to get her killed—' Tristram broke cover.

'Stay back—' Red sprang after him, bringing Tristram down in a cloud of soot. Tristram began to struggle, both of them freezing as the hollow *crump... crump...* of a mortar began to hammer against the sides of the church, each new explosion bounding over the shoulders of the last, fusillade doubling, growing manic as the dirigible pawed the ground with searchlights and the aeroplanes mobbed the hilltop, machine guns cackling.

'Madness,' Tristram screamed, 'utter madness.'

'Delightful, I think.' Nox strolled towards them, his nighttime walk accompanied by Floyd and another bodyguard. 'Don't you think this is beautiful, Tristram?' Nox embraced the gouts of flame, the clamour of gunfire, applauding as a grenade exploded.

The brigade stepped out into the open, firing wildly, some of the gangers jeering, or laughing, none of them noticing the first passing rush of air. None noticing the first gangster's scream, the line moving forward, unawares as another ducked, fired wildly into the darkness and, next instant, was knocked to the dirt.

The night grew wings. Grew talons, and sharp beaks of obsidian.

'Attack,' bellowed Nox, still laughing, 'don't stop.'

The night reached out and struck his shoulder, pitching him over. Floyd shot into the air. Too late, another shape already condensing out of the black.

A raven.

Tristram ducked, downdraft of wings passing raking his neck.

Crouching, Red fired into a flock of magpies mobbing one of the mortar crews, only for another shadow to fall, talons outstretched, towards him. Tristram knocked Red out of its path and the crow banked steeply, screeching as it turned to try again.

'Fall back.' Tristram yelled at Nox, jabbing a finger towards the house on the edge of the waste. 'Pull your men back, Nox.'

'Never.' Nox snatched the pistol from Floyd's hand. 'Forwards,' he screamed, firing madly into the sky, 'forwards.'

Stars appeared, flickering in the blackness lurking inside the ruined church, light slithering around broken walls and over the lip of scarred window frames, stained carmine and rust where any of the window glass remained, or shedding beacon light from the top of the bell tower: dozens, hundreds of candle flames guttering into life. With the light came snarling, the snap of new shapes weaving between the gangsters, fangs nipping, biting deep.

Red took aim; Floyd, tugging a heavy revolver from a second holster beneath his coat, opened fire. But the dogs were as dark and swift as the birds, little more than fresh smoke on a wind swift and lithe. Tristram bellowed at Nox but there was no space for reason amidst the crack of pistol shots, the stutter of machine gun fire ending on a scream. Another crow's swoop forced him to his knees. He pressed his hands to his ears, wanting a moment's silence and finding the battle trying to weave the thud of his heart into its own jagged pulse. Tristram crouched lower, turning away from the church and the flash of gunfire, seeing a tiny shape swerve and bob: too small for a magpie or crow, there and gone again.

No time to think. Tristram chased after the sparrow.

A black sun.

'She's gone.'

A famished moon.

'Dead,' another told him as they trudged across no-man's-land, dozens of soldiers plodding towards the black sun buried in the horizon. Crows hung from rusting barbed wire, a dismal breeze scraping against the loops and snagging the clouds on the remaining tree stumps and the shards of plank wall peering out of the deserted trenches. The battle lines had dissolved, forgotten, all purpose lost with her death.

'She means everything,' one of the soldiers slogging through the mire told Tristram.

'What year is this?'

The soldier shrugged. '1919, sir.'

The breeze whimpered but could not hide the ticking of the black sun as it cooled.

'The war's never going to end now,' the soldier said.

'But—'

The moon fell in on itself, one crescent tip pricking a hole in the sky. A trickle of light escaped, groping until it found the cortège trundling between morass and shell hole.

'It doesn't mean nothing, sir.' The soldier tugged at Tristram's sleeve, urging him to keep walking. 'It's too late for them.'

A phalanx of mounted knights lumbered at the head of the procession, armour tarnished, their pennants—black sun and famished moon—stained and tattered.

'Don't pay them no mind, sir,' the soldier advised.

Sullen mourners straggled behind the knights, some in formal black or Sunday best, others in uniform or their everyday clothes. Heads bowed, they walked in silence, as did the seven roan horses dragging the hearse behind them. The black sun heaved itself free of the horizon and reeled over the mourners' heads to settle above the rear of the cortège, its sombre light finding Vivien, a bride in black lace and taffeta following the procession.

'There's no point to this, sir.' The soldier plucked at Tristram's sleeve. 'She's dead, ain't she?'

'But she's not.' Tristram waded frantically through the mud, calling to her. But Vivien ignored him, as did the knights and mourners. Only the groom carrying the bride's long train turned, his face hidden beneath veils of black, white and yellow lace.

'How can you?' Tristram demanded. 'How can you take part in this grotesque—' He peered at the veils. 'Aubrey? Is that—? Dammit, Villiers, you—'

He snatched away the veil.

Not Aubrey. Nor Villiers, not anyone. Except, on second thoughts, the eyes and the mouth reminded him of himself, older and weather-beaten by bitterness and exhaustion, soul eaten away by cynicism.

'I'm dead, Tristram, don't prate on so,' Vivien yawned.

The black sun began to shed snow, black flakes tumbling.

'I would have loved you,' Tristram murmured, looking into the groom's face.

'What about the little princess with the pretty little locket?'

'She wanted me to help her, it's—'

'You don't love her?'

'I want to be faithful to your memory.'

'Oh.' Vivien waved for the mourners and knights to start walking again. 'Well, if that's what you want, Tristram, but don't keep bothering me with it all.'

The groom pushed past him and Tristram slipped, falling into the ooze, sporadic gunfire beginning to sound in the distance, shadows yawing as the black sun likewise lost its grip on the sky and flopped to earth, its dimming half-light catching a glimmer of red quickly swallowed by another gout of smoke, smoke drawing aside to reveal an ember in the twilight, part vermilion, part scarlet.

Her dress was too thin for the cold and the mud. 'Go back.' Tristram floundered, ooze drawing him deeper as he strained to find something solid to push against. 'Go,' he told her.

The woman in vermilion and scarlet knelt and took his hand, pulling, slipping, trying again. The mud dragged them both into its grasp, only loose hold itself, Tristram and the woman in vermilion and scarlet helping each other escape to firmer ground. The woman barely took time to gasp breath before she began rubbing warmth into his arms. She began to shiver herself and Tristram clumsily tried to chafe her hands and shoulders in turn, remembering how stern and unforgiving she had seemed as she had climbed from the flask.

He wrapped his arms around her, rubbing her back before simply holding her as he searched for the right question, for anything to say, dismissing everything until there was nothing to do but hold this frail woman in vermilion and scarlet. Until he heard the sparrow's song. Until a submachine gun barked and fell silent.

Tristram looked up.

A raven struck his head.

Flutter of wings merging into the drag of skirts across the charred ground, raven's caw sounding familiar, a voice not expected to be heard again. A pistol shot interrupted, ricochet drowned by laughter that was also the barking of dogs and the cackle of magpie and crow, the hiss of an alley cat, chortling.

'He's waiting.'

Pain worked a deeper into his forehead, tearing his eyes, tears smudging the lights from the church into waves that brushed against the smoke clouds, encouraging black to become amber. A wind soughed, arrogant and presumptuous. It huffed and blustered, raising jeers and laughter, and the wind was Nox's voice, tone growing haughtier, bringing more laughter and so growing more imperious.

'Don't loll about, *Uram* Tristram.'

A boot toe nudged him. Raven wings, raven skirts: Sára leaned closer. Raven black fluttering. Tristram saw Floyd, handing out threats but careful not to make any sudden moves, a woman in charcoal pressing a carving knife to his throat.

That was Kata.

And Éva and Dorottya guarded Nox, ignoring his demands and orders. He no longer had a private army, simply a brigade of prisoners, captured by thieves and pickpockets, hoodlums and brawlers—people like themselves only poorer and less organised, the kinds of people Tristram recognised from the streets around Raven Passage.

Sára nudged him again. 'Up, *Uram* Tristram, he's waiting.' She heaved him to his feet and pointed towards the church. 'He's expecting you.'

Garlands, white and yellow, in peony and rose. Hanging from singed walls and every pew still able to carry the weight. The church was dressed for a wedding.

The last of the gangsters was made to sit, bride's side of the nave packed and just two places left on the groom's side.

'This is madness,' Tristram hissed as they squeezed on to the end of the bench. Sára made no reply.

The lights peppered along the walls and remaining roof beams, swelled as even more candles sparked into life around the altar, turning white petals into gold, yellow petals glistening with the colours of sunset. A smell of orange blossom filled the air.

The congregation fidgeted, rustle of conversation expectant as it wandered the church, pointing out Nox, Floyd beside him on the front row, Mátyás seated behind them, his elbows resting on the back of their pew as he leaned forward, deep into a one-sided conversation that Nox pointedly ignored. Tristram spotted Anna and Terézia in the rows behind him, and the old men, still hiding behind their moustaches as they passed a bottle along the pew, each taking a nip; spotting Dorottya the pew behind them, the barman perched beside her. Most of the guests were strangers, however, candlelight offering a glimpse of another face on the off chance it was someone he knew, light dancing away almost at once, shadows leaping to give the impression this guest had the head of a crow, that a magpie, this one a fox or a dog.

Red sat at the end of the front pew beside Nox and Floyd. He swivelled in his seat, staring around the church until he caught sight of Tristram. They exchanged a glance.

A breeze leapt to its feet, ruffling the garlands, petals clapping together, that clapping taken up by the guests.

'Greetings!'

Voit stepped from behind a screen across the end of the chancel. The clapping grew louder.

'Greetings,' he proclaimed again, arms spread in welcome. The breeze applauded, pausing to tug admiringly at his robes, holding them out for the candlelight to touch: gold and silver embroidery; the face of the Moon, the face of the Sun. Here an Empress, there an Emperor. And twin serpents coiling around sleeves of midnight and noon, black and white.

Voit enjoyed the applause a little longer before approaching the congregation. Nox stiffened. Voit smiled, delighted. He clapped his hands.

Silence.

'And greetings to you, dear cousin Nox.'

Nox lunged. Casually, Mátyás snatched a handful of coat collar and slammed Nox against the back of the pew. Floyd tried to defend his boss but one of the brawlers sitting beside Mátyás slapped his face, another brawler flourishing a short length of fence post, nails hammered crudely through its head, until Floyd subsided.

'We are not cousins,' Nox insisted, trying to smooth his collar and composure, and giving up on both. 'We are nothing,' he snapped. 'How dare you, you—'

Mátyás slapped Nox across the back of the head, reminding him that fat people didn't get to have opinions.

Voit's smile deepened. 'It is ever a delight to be in your company, my dearest Nox. And, it is an even greater delight to have the company of you all—' Voit stood back and opened his arms, the church filling with cheers and clapping— 'for this joyous union. A wedding, my dearest friends and companions, a wedding of soul and of spirit, of Luna and Sol. This evening, shall we not conjoin the realms of psyche and the earthly? Shall we not enjoy great reward and greater riches?'

Applause, cheers, shouts: the cackling of magpies, the

caw of crows, the beat of paw against paw, hand against hand.

'Dearest friends,' Voit called out.

Tristram looked away from the congregation, a cold sweat deepening. He tried not to look at Sára in case she was also part human, part spirit.

'Yes, all these fine things will be ours this evening, dearest friends.' Voit hushed the congregation. 'All, if... if...' Voit came closer. 'If you, dearest Tristram, will be so kind as to give me what has been mine all along.'

Tristram had no idea what he meant.

Voit smiled, benign patience. 'But, of course, the locket, my so very good friend, the locket that is the very root of this delightful escapade that is our friendship.'

'I don't have—'

'You,' Voit bellowed. 'Do. You do,' he screamed, candles leaping and the breeze lashing against the walls, garlands bending, their petals turning black, next moment blanching as Voit's demeanour returned to its supremely urbane and poised self.

'But it was entrusted into your safe keeping, brother Tristram,' he explained sweetly.

'It is mine.' Nox wormed out of Mátyás's grip. 'It belongs to neither of you. It's mine.' Nox dashed spittle from his mouth. He stood and brushed down his coat, slicking back his hair. 'Mine,' he repeated, tone almost normal.

'As you wish, cousin.' Voit looked bored. 'But, since I have you both, I will have the locket.'

'No.' Nox sounded quiet matter of fact.

'But yes, cousin.' Voit pointed: beyond the walls, the darkness and, beyond the darkness, the restless glow of a hundred fires, each fire joined into a single blaze that, little by little, ate Buda and would soon cross to Pest. 'The fire is mine. It follows my will. As will you, all of you. Else every thing,' Voit emphasised, 'burns.'

Nox raised an eyebrow. 'Let it.'

'Very well.' Voit stepped back and, although he made neither sign nor gesture, the breeze died and the whole church fell silent.

Alba stepped around the screen, wedding white, her gown glowing in the light of so many candles. Reluctantly, she approached until she was almost at Voit's side.

Tristram sprang to his feet. Alba's gaze flickered towards him.

'My wife to be,' Voit announced, turning his smile on Nox last of all. 'What do you say now, dearest cousin?'

There was fear in her gaze, of course, but Tristram saw something else, there and gone in a moment.

Sára stood, blocking his way to the aisle before he realised he had taken a step.

'She is not yours.' Nox thrust a hand into his coat pocket, pulling it free before Mátyás or anyone else had chance to reach him. All expecting a gun and confounded by the length of fine silver and gold chain that hung from Nox's fingers.

'This makes her mine.'

Nox looped the chain between both hands and tugged.

Alba gasped, knees giving way.

Nox twisted the links.

Alba bit back a scream, clutching at her ankle.

Nox wrenched at the chain again. Alba clenched her jaw, staring at Nox and trying not to react.

Sára's hand pressed into Tristram's chest, pushing him back. He would have argued but her expression made him stand, fists tight pressed to his mouth.

'*My* wife.' Nox pushed the chain under Voit's nose.

'But—' Voit laughed. 'But, cousin, you can never consummate the marriage, can you?'

'You filthy—' Nox screwed up the chain, unable to speak. Alba screamed. Neither man took any notice.

'The divine Alba is mine, dearest Nox. All this is—' Voit waved a finger towards the restless gangsters, the garlanded church— 'is beside the point. Spirit and soul, Nox, do you see?' He raised a hand.

The candle flames leapt eagerly. The fires in the city roared in ecstasy, leaping over themselves, turning the night into a furnace.

Voit's smile became a laugh. 'Rather a pleasing effect, wouldn't you say, cousin?'

Nox trembled, the stones beneath the church shaking in sympathy. The rumble of engines grew thunderous and the leviathan shape of the dirigible peered down through the broken roof, a dozen aeroplanes mobbing the space around it.

'I will bomb.'

As his mouth moved, Nox's words came out in the clash of engine.

'The street you called home, Voit, and the ones around it. That charming bar.' Nox turned until he saw the barman. 'Every street where your... associates live.'

The candles shrank, darkness scuttling.

'I will bomb the whole of Pest.' The engines grew more strident. 'The whole of Buda.' Words deafening. 'Everything. All of it. None of it matters, only that I get what is mine.'

As Nox spoke, the gangsters slid from their pews, knuckledusters and coshes, straight razors and lead pipes appearing from hidden pockets, the gangsters re-arming themselves, ready to fight again. And, in turn, Voit's followers began to fold into the shadows waiting beneath the candles. A dog snarled out into the light, a crow sprang from the gloom, cackling. A cat hissed.

Tristram found himself pushing Sára aside. He managed half a step before the pressure of a knife at his throat brought him to a halt.

'A blessèd event, *mon cher Capitaine*,' the curé mumbled, taking the knife away long enough to indicate the open doorway. 'After you.'

The old parish church looked as Tristram remembered it, even the distant rumble of artillery and the smell of cognac on the curé's breath was the same. Garlands of flowers felt sorry for themselves as they hung dejectedly along the nave, midnight-blue petals sucking the last warmth out of the air, the congregation shivering over orders of service.

A harmonium wheezed as the curé waved Tristram to the front of the church, music stumbling over a discord and falling silent: a drunkard's fanfare to welcome Vivien, black lace and taffeta, walking down the aisle with the veiled man on her arm.

'Do you,' the curé asked Tristram, 'give away this woman into a state of flesh?'

'I—' Tristram pressed his hands to his head. 'I don't understand.'

The veiled man pulled the covering from his face, revealing features that were unformed, always mutable.

'I don't want any of this,' Tristram told Vivien, unsure whether, this time, he was to be the father of the bride or the groom himself.

'You don't want to be mine?' Vivien fumbled in her black reticule, swaying and cursing, drunk as the curé. 'Isn't this what you want?' She found a wedding band, swearing as she almost lost hold of it. 'It is,' she told him, clutching his hand and trying to jam the ring on to his finger.

Tristram flinched. Pain lanced up his arm, winding serpent's coils around him. The stones of the old church moaned. The trees and the grass and the clouds nearby groaned in pain. For an eternity, it seemed it was his pain alone. In the next instant, Tristram felt the stone's pain, the pain of the stars beyond the clouds. He knew a woodlouse's pain, as it clung to one of the beams, could feel the terror of a field mouse caught in a shaft of moonlight, these pains shared between them all.

One of the congregation laughed, derisive and cynical. Another clapped, others joining in as the harmonium slurred over the Wedding March, the happy couple staggering down the aisle, the assembly clomping out after them. The curé threw an arm around Tristram's shoulder, kissing his cheek before tottering away.

The harmonium was abruptly silent.

A hand rested against his arm. Tristram turned towards the woman in vermilion and scarlet.

She looked cold and exhausted. But she squeezed his shoulder again, trying to comfort him.

'I'm sorry.'

It took a moment for him to know what he meant by this. Tristram hesitated, picturing her pushing him away. But when he hugged her, she hugged him back.

'I'm sorry,' he said again, the words themselves meaningless, or meaning more than they appeared to. Tristram held the woman in vermilion and scarlet more tightly, comforting her as she comforted him, mumbling words that meant more in this moment than they might at any other time, kissing her gently, kisses returned: left cheek, right cheek, left again before once on the lips, the sparrow singing very close by as the woman in vermilion and scarlet held him and he held the woman, sparrow's song not quite fading as a knife blade pressed against Tristram's throat.

'Balls,' Voit was saying. He laughed. 'You don't have them, dear Nox.'

The knife dug deeper, blade trembling as Sára looked from Voit to Nox. She glanced at Tristram and eased the pressure of the flick knife a fraction. Fists clenched with the effort not to move suddenly or too far, he snatched a breath.

'Don't,' Nox hissed, raising a hand. 'Don't push me again.'

His hand fell.

Light into flame into sound, explosion bounding across the charred waste, candle flames shying from the noise. Another bomb detonated close by, a third caught up in the shriek of aeroplanes and the leviathan rumble of the dirigible.

'Shut up,' Voit yelled.

A dog snarled.

Sára took away the knife. The sound of it moving might have been the song of a bird. She looked at Tristram, the hard shell, jaded and indifferent, she so often hid behind cracking.

He lifted his hand, fist still clenched.

'Isn't this what you're both looking for?' He stepped into the aisle, Sára following him as he called out to Voit and Nox.

Tristram opened his hand. 'Isn't it?'

The locket looked far too ordinary to be the source of all this.

'Give that to me, dearest Tristram.'

Voit managed a few steps before Nox tried to grab his arm, Floyd bounding forward, quickly followed by Mátyás, Red also on his feet, hesitating, glancing from Nox to Tristram.

Shadows scurried, drawing breath and weapons, tense with expectation.

Tristram took another step.

Nox pushed Voit aside. 'Give me that,' he snapped.

'What will you give me?' The air clotted around the locket. Tristram managed another step. 'If I do?'

'Your life.' Nox raise his hand. The aeroplanes and dirigible answered.

'Don't listen to him, dearest Tristram.' Voit heaved Alba to her feet. 'I offer you everything you've ever wanted.'

'Do not part with it, Tristram.' Alba struggled against Voit. 'They are both liars—'

'I am not bluffing,' Nox insisted, raising his hand.

'Nor am I.' Tristram made to dash the locket across the flagstones. Voit and Nox froze but, when Tristram motioned for Alba to come to him, Voit relaxed, pushing her forward as he stretched out his other hand.

'Stay where you are.' Nox brandished the chain. 'Alba, come to me. Tristram can then hand me the lock—'

'Do not listen to them, Tristram,' Alba warned, caught in a no-man's-land between Tristram and Nox, Nox and Voit. 'Keep the locket.'

'No—' Tristram swung his arm downwards.

Nox and Voit shrieked, staggering from the blow of impact. A blow that had not landed.

Only a moment's confusion before they realised Tristram had not let go of the locket, but long enough for Tristram to pull Alba to him.

'Do you want it?' He held open his hand.

'No.' Alba shook her head. 'Not in the least, but…'

'Well, what do you want?' Tristram raised his voice to be heard over Voit and Nox's threats and complaints.

Alba shook her head. 'To be free of this, I suppose.'

Tristram closed his fingers over the locket. 'Then you don't need this. You can be free without it, Alba.' She shook her head and he nodded: 'I think you can.'

Reluctant, she hesitated before kneeling unsteadily to take hold of the silver and gold chain around her ankle.

Time lost hold of the ruined church, let the twin cities of Buda and Pest slip from its grasp. Birds paused on the wing. Each fire waited, flames turning towards the scorched waste ground and the remains of the church. Hearts continued to beat, only the space between this beat and the next became unfixed, infinite if that was how long it took Alba to break the chain.

Tristram felt Sára somewhere beside him, Nox and Voit caught in mid-leap, faces contorted in the midst of ordering Alba to stop, Floyd and Mátyás there somewhere, too, Red visible on the periphery, face caught between emotions. Only Alba mattered. Only Alba moved, shoulders and arms shaking as she strained against the links of silver and gold, an effort that might go on forever, from which no one might be released.

The chain snapped.

Breath. Movement. Voit and Nox catching themselves, babbling orders, the room gathering itself to leap.

Red moved first.

Swearing as he grabbed Nox and pressed a revolver to his employer's forehead. 'Stop this crap.' Tightening his grip, he pushed the muzzle harder. Nox muttered under his breath. 'Stop this now.'

'Certainly, my dear young friend.' Voit beckoned for

Mátyás to take charge of Nox. 'It's good of you to help—'

'Don't try that—'

'Or you'll shoot my cousin? Capital! Mátyás—'

Voit choked. A shadow slid about his shoulders. Shadow an arm, a hand, a knife at his throat.

Sára stood beside him, raven-black amidst jittering candle light. 'I might slip,' she whispered, 'if you squirm and fight. Slip many, many times.'

'Tristram?' Alba held up the loose links of silver and gold.

'Try,' he suggested and she cupped the chain in her hands, concentrating, a few seconds at most, before she opened her hands and the locket lay in her palm. Tristram rested his hand over hers, hands rising, swift and certain.

The locket dashed across the flagstones.

Voit's scream became Nox's scream, the screams the beating of wings, crows and rooks, jackdaws and magpies, whirlwinds of feathers, so fast they blurred, loosing form and colour, becoming flurries more white than black, air churned by the barking of dogs and foxes, alley cats' shrilling, uproar consuming the beat of engine and propeller.

Alba pulled him into the lee of one of the pews. Tristram caught glimpses of Nox and Voit scrambling across the floor after any shard or scrap of the locket, remains scattered wider by the beat of wings and thrashing paws, by gangsters and street bruisers running in frenzied circles, shouting, tripping over, treading on Nox's fingers or Voit's, skidding, kicking away yet another fragment of enamel or gold.

'That way.' Voit pointed, voice almost lost in the din.

There was nothing in the direction Voit pointed. Perhaps a flitter of white, though that might have been anything, or nothing. And yet Nox was already on his feet, pointing, the two men barging against each other as they ran. Others following after them. On foot, or paw, on wings of black and white. Taking up the call and plunging into the darkness. Nox's voice indistinguishable from Voit's, voices quickly lost, leaving the drum of foot and wing, the beat of propellers, planes making a final circle as the last stragglers careered over the scorched ground to disappear into the streets beyond, dirigible already lumbering after Voit and Nox, shrouds of smoke and cloud closing behind it, a few gaps opening directly overhead as they did so, a handful of stars peering down on the remains of the church where silence now sat amongst the pews and the wreckage.

'Holy shit.'

Red pressed a hand across his mouth, face waxen. He was beginning to shake.

'Holy shit,' he whispered.

Sára laughed, closing the flick knife and slipping it within the folds of her midnight dress. With a flurry of skirts, she offered Tristram and Alba a deep curtsey.

'*Uram* Tristram...' Sára laughed again, picking a way through the broken pews, waving once as she chose a path in another direction entirely to Nox and Voit.

'Er... Miss?' Red stumbled after Sára. 'Miss? I don't know this town, you got somewhere in mind to— Miss?' Sára made no reply. But she waited until he caught up.

The night closed its arms around them.

'Thank you.'

Alba kissed his cheek a second time. She smiled, sitting back on her heels and opening her hand, the locket tarnished and scuffed but whole once again.

'You don't need that, you know.'

'I know.' Alba stood, shaking the worst of the soot and grime from her wedding gown. 'But I don't want from it what Nox wants. Or Voit.' Very carefully, she tucked the locket away. 'Or you, Tristram.'

He wanted to ask her what she meant and what she knew but it felt like the wrong time. He stood and watched as Alba chose a direction as different from the one Voit and Nox had taken as it was from the way Sára and Red had followed.

'Take care,' Tristram called as she stepped over the threshold of the church and faded from view.

The first spots of rain speckled the flagstones, setting the remaining candles to hissing, lights guttering as the downpour gained strength. Tristram tilted his head, the rain washing his face, certain, when he looked again, he could see stars overhead, rain falling from a clear sky.

V
SOLVE ET
COAGULUM

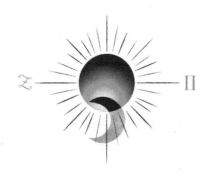

IT WAS STILL raining when he woke.

Flint clouds grew threadbare over the rooftops, drizzle fading while the sun peeked out only to hide, unsure whether it wanted to show itself yet. Kazinczy utca lay slick under the night's heavy rain, and the bushes and trees in the walled garden dripped. The noise of motorcars and a thousand people bustling through their mornings seemed hushed, muted by the flutter of wings as ten pigeons rose from the trees to circle and vanish behind the house. Tristram leaned further out the bedroom window, searching the sky to the east and finding nothing but pearlescent cloud, rain's scent on the wind.

The house was quiet silent, tailor's dummies making no comment as he went down to the kitchen. Fresh bread, a pan of porridge warming at the back of the range, hot tea in the pot: no other sign of Rózsa.

But, later, it was a few minutes walk at most to find Tiresias, stationed on a corner, the felt hat on the pavement before him. Neither spoke as Tristram sat and watched the street, the passers-by, realising Spring was walking amongst them for the first time, its hand sometimes guiding someone to take out a few coins and drop them into the hat. Tristram nodded thank you.

And so morning passed into afternoon, and afternoon began to speak of dinner, of an evening beside the fire because, no matter that the sun had found a way between the clouds, it would be a cool night. Tristram stirred, about to suggest he and Tiresias go back to the house, when someone paused by the hat.

Dove grey trousers. And white spats, marred by a single smirch.

Tristram searched out the fray on the man's left cuff. And looked into the landlord's kindly face. The landlord gave a nod as he gently took Tristram's hand and folded over his fingers, tight and safe.

Without a word, gone again, lost amongst the late afternoon crowd, the landlord leaving Tristram to study his closed hand, sure, already, what was inside, although it was easy to doubt, it had been so quick. And, of course, when he did open his hand, there was the locket. Gold quite brilliant and enamel no longer cracked, Sun and Moon inside as clear as Hermes, who raised a finger to his lips, the journey not yet over.